COMHAIRLE CHONTAE ROSCOMÁIN
LEABHARLANNA CHONTAE ROSCOMÁIN

1. This book may be retained for three weeks.
2. This book may be renewed if not requested
   by another borrower.
   ...nes on overdue books will be charged by
   ...ue notices.

04 4.	RCL

BRYAN MALESSA

The Flight

FOURTH ESTATE • *London*

First published in Great Britain in 2007 by
Fourth Estate
An imprint of HarperCollins*Publishers*
77–85 Fulham Palace Road
London W6 8JB
www.4thestate.co.uk

1

A catalogue record for this book is
available from the British Library

ISBN-13 978-0-00-724106-4
ISBN-10 0-00-724106-2

Typeset in Minion by Palimpsest Book Production Limited,
Grangemouth, Stirlingshire

Printed in Great Britain by Clays Ltd, St Ives plc

This book is proudly printed on paper which contains wood
from well-managed forests, certified in accordance with
the rules of the Forest Stewardship Council.
For more information about FSC,
please visit www.fsc-uk.org

for my family

BOOK I

Samland

Chapter 1

On 15 June 1940 a celebration took place on the small *Platz*, the square, in Germau in front of Karl's parents' shop. The previous evening's radio broadcast had carried news of victory in Paris. The villagers nervously set up their goods to sell, hopeful that victory would quickly translate to peace. Early that morning Ida had asked her father, Landwirt, who had walked over from his village, to slaughter one of the few remaining pigs for the party. He wasn't much good at butchering, but she couldn't worry about that today: she was preoccupied with thoughts of her absent husband.

She knew Paul was safe on the outskirts of Paris where he had been sent to ensure a steady supply of food for the troops. When he had received his call-up papers he had closed their butchery because Ida hadn't the strength or the skill to run the slaughterhouse, and the children – Karl, Peter and Leyna – were too young to train. No one in the village, including Paul, had thought it a matter for concern; everyone was certain that the war would be short and the soldiers would return as heroes. The decisive victory in Paris seemed to confirm that Paul would soon be home, she thought, as she sat on the front steps of the shop, which was also their home. Adults had gathered round the linden tree, encircled by an ornate iron railing that stood in the centre of the village square. A group of children were playing hide and seek near the trees surrounding the village, oblivious to their parents' worries.

Suddenly Karl, her oldest, appeared from the group, sprinting towards her. He came through the gate that separated the shop from the square and sat down, panting, beside her. When he could speak, it was to ask again the question he had repeated since last evening's broadcast: 'When is Father coming home?'

At first she looked at him without speaking; then she said, 'Come here.' She wiped a smudge of dirt from his cheek with her apron. 'I told you to stop asking.'

'But Salomo says he's dead.'

Ida looked out at her neighbour's son chasing Leyna through the trees. She could hear them giggling. 'Tell Salomo I'll spank him myself if he says that again.'

'When do we eat?'

'Soon. Go and look after your little sister.'

Karl jumped up and ran back through the gate. As he crossed the square he stumbled on a loose cobble, then continued, darting through a group of adults. He ignored his sister and ran up the path to the church that stood at the top of a hill to see if he could spot Peter, his younger brother.

The village where Ida's father lived, Sorgenau, was a few kilometres west of Germau, close to the amber town of Palmnicken. Landwirt had moved there with his Lithuanian bride shortly after Ida's mother had died of cancer two years earlier. The roads that led to Germau dated from as far back as the Bronze Age, when the indigenous Balt-Prussians had traded their only precious resource, amber, with the outside world in exchange for metal to use in jewellery, tools and weapons. For centuries the region had remained so remote that although Tacitus and Ptolemy had mentioned it in their writings, Pliny the Elder referred mistakenly to the Samland peninsula as an island: Amber Island. Like the shards of amber that washed up daily on the local beaches, there were other bits and pieces of rarely mentioned history that marked the region: on conquering Samland seven centuries earlier the Teutonic Knights had stolen the non-Germanic tribe's name and used it to christen their own empire. Prussia rose as one of the most militant and chauvinistic of all German states, despite the fact that many of the assimilated Baltic Prussians, including Ida's clan, silently traced their names and lineage to a pre-Germanic past. But on that summer afternoon in 1940, no one was thinking about the village's history as they gathered on the *Platz* to sing, laugh, drink, dance and make merry in honour of the news they had heard on the radio.

Ida, though, wasn't quite ready to join the party and remained apart, nervously fingering her bracelet as she watched Karl reach the ancient church the Knights had built above the village.

'Have you seen the sharpening stone?' a voice called behind her.

She turned. Her father had come out of the slaughterhouse, cleaning a knife on a piece of cloth. When he saw her face he said, 'I told you, you've nothing to worry about.' He hobbled over to her and sat down beside her – always a struggle with his wooden leg. He'd lost his own defending East Prussia from the Russians in 1914 at the battle of Tannenberg. 'Paul will be fine. The army's in control. It will be over soon.'

Ida knew he wasn't telling her what she wanted to hear. 'It's in the kitchen,' she said, 'in the drawer to the right of the sink.'

Landwirt grabbed the iron railing and pulled himself up again.

'I'll tell one of the children to clean the slaughterhouse,' she said. 'Go and join the men when you've finished. I must start cooking.'

'We'll do it together, over the fire pit. It's you who should join the party. Come on! Up!' He spoke to her as if she were still a child, but she stood up and straightened her dress, forced herself to smile and went out on to the square.

'Ida!'

Romy, Salomo's mother, was coming towards her. Landwirt rolled his eyes and turned away.

'Mr Badura was just telling me you managed to buy some cloth when you went to Königsberg last week. I was wondering if you had any left over – I'm trying to finish a blanket for my cousin. She's expecting next month.'

'I think there's a little. I'll have a look later.'

'I don't suppose you'd do it now? I wanted to finish it tonight and we might miss each other this evening.'

Ida went into her home and located the rest of the cloth with which she had made Leyna a new dress.

'Can I give you something for it?' Romy asked when Ida handed it to her.

'There's no need. My best wishes to your cousin. Now I must help my father with the pig.'

'Would you like my help?'

'The slaughterhouse is too small for a crowd,' Ida said. 'We'll catch up later, after we've eaten.'

When Romy had gone Ida started to close the door but saw Leyna running through the gate, so she opened it again. 'Mutti, Salomo's teasing me! When are we going to eat?'

'I wish you and Karl would stop asking that.'

They walked through the house and out of the back door where they found Landwirt smoking and gazing into the pasture.

'You call that work?' Ida joked.

He dropped the cigarette, grabbed Leyna and flung her into the air as she shrieked with delight, 'Put me down, Grandpa!'

Soon a side of pork was roasting over the open pit beside the slaughterhouse where a group of men had gathered. Each generation had its favourite songs and as the afternoon wore on the villagers began to sing. Even the boys on the square stopped playing and started to sing a Hitler Youth song they had learned from the older boys at school:

> We march for Hitler through the night.
> Suffering with the flag for freedom and bread.
> Our flag means more to us than death . . .

The old men, all veterans of the last war, laughed bitterly. 'What do they know about death?' one muttered.

Another called, 'Go and get us some of the bread you're singing about. We haven't finished eating yet.'

The children were silent – until they realised that the men were laughing at them. Then they sang even louder:

> We march for Hitler through the night.
> Suffering with the flag for freedom . . .

Chapter 2

That autumn, each Thursday after lunch, Karl, Peter and Leyna waited on the hill outside the village beside the road that led to Fischhausen. From there they could see nearly two kilometres down the long straight road as they looked for the postman, trying to guess when he would appear. The younger two had to rely on their brother's word because he wouldn't let them see the watch their grandfather had given him.

Once they were certain the postman was on his way, they sprinted into the woods, along the path and down the hill, across a glade and back up the opposite hill to the church. When they reached the cemetery they stopped to catch their breath, then ran down into the square just before the truck arrived.

They wanted to be ready in case their father had sent them a parcel. They were the only children in Germau who received sweets in the post each month, but they waited for the postman each week in case he had sent an extra one. Ida made them open it at home – otherwise, she knew, they'd eat it all at once. Each evening, after they had done their piano practice, she would give them a little until everything had been eaten. The children took their daily ration outside to where the others waited.

When a picture appeared in the newspaper of soldiers marching along the Champs Élysées towards the Arc de Triomphe, Karl cut it out and, in the field beside the church, showed it to the other village children, saying that his father was among the soldiers at the rear. Peter supported him although both knew that Paul hadn't marched into the city with the troops. Karl refused to share his sweets with two boys who didn't believe him. 'Who else would have sent us chocolate from Paris?' Karl asked.

The boys considered this and agreed it must have been his father. He rewarded them with a nibble that seemed more delicious than anything German.

'Maybe my father will go to Italy,' one said, 'and send us something even better.'

'Italy's already on our side, stupid. They'll probably send him to Africa where they don't have sweets.'

By now they'd eaten what Ida had given them.

'See if your mother will give you more,' one boy said.

'She won't. She said it's almost gone.'

'Let's go and look for the secret tunnel, then.'

Immediately the children forgot about Paris and ran off. Mr Wolff had once told Karl about a tunnel that, long ago, monks had dug beneath the church. It opened somewhere in the woods and offered a last means of escape to those besieged in the building. It had rarely been used, however, since the time of the Teutonic Knights who had trained with arms and studied military strategy with the same devotion they showed to the Virgin Mary. Mr Wolff, the local coffin maker, enjoyed sharing his knowledge of their home with the children. 'Everyone should know their history,' he would say.

One afternoon when Karl and Peter had stood near the doorway to his shop, listening to his stories, Mr Wolff had pulled a stone from his coat pocket. Karl had recognised it as amber – *Bernstein*. 'The church was once used as the headquarters where amber disputes were settled,' Mr Wolff told them. 'Most of the world's amber comes from around here.'

'Then why aren't we rich?' Karl asked.

'You're richer than many people. You need not worry about what others think of you.'

'What do you mean?' Karl asked.

Mr Wolff ignored his question. Instead he told the boys that long before the church had been designated the Amber Palace, a Jewish trader had been the second person in recorded history to mention the Prussian tribe living on the Baltic coast. Ibrâhim ibn-Ya'qub had travelled to the region from Spain and recorded his findings in Arabic.

With the baker, Mr Schultze, whose shop stood opposite the butcher's, Mr Wolff was the only other Jewish person remaining in the village. Of the two, only Mr Schultze had married – a Protestant woman from the capital. In the years after Hitler had been elected to power, the four other Jewish families in Germau had followed the example of those in Königsberg and fled to safer countries. Karl had once overheard his father asking Mr Wolff whether it was wise for him to remain in Germany.

'This is home. Where else would I go?' Mr Wolff had replied.

The villagers came to him occasionally as the arbiter in their never-ending disputes over obscure historical events. Since leaving home in his early twenties, Mr Wolff had distanced himself from his religion and focused on the study of history, convinced that intellectual and spiritual pursuits led to a similar end: self-knowledge and inner peace. In his early thirties he had reconsidered his rejection of formal religion after studying the Reformation. Instead of returning to Judaism, though, he had become interested in Protestantism. He didn't formally convert, but he attended services occasionally and had even led Christians in prayer – for the first time when a family had requested he deliver a coffin to their farm. When he arrived, the widow asked if he would say a few words for her deceased husband, before helping them bury him in the family plot. He had been honoured by her request.

On the afternoon that Paul had asked him whether it was wise to remain in Germany, he had also asked Mr Wolff who he expected would help him if trouble came. The coffin maker had frowned and made no answer. As time passed, he noticed that the villagers who had once expressed independent views now accepted each new policy without question. It had begun back in 1934 with the banning of Jewish holidays from German calendars. In 1935 Mr Wolff had been excluded from the Armed Forces and forbidden to fly the German flag – which had hurt: he had always been among the first in Germau to raise it on national holidays. Then his citizenship was revoked, in line with the Nuremberg Laws, and in 1936 his assets were taxed an additional twenty-five per cent – all because of his religious heritage.

The villagers' acceptance of each new law through the years was unsettling enough, but then, in the months following Paul's blunt and unsettling question, Mr Wolff had noticed that friends with whom he had always been on good terms slowly began to distance themselves. The days Mr Wolff had once spent busy with work and the evenings once occupied visiting friends were soon replaced by long idle hours alone, the social life he had once cherished slowly withering away to nothing. Although Mr Wolff enjoyed spending time alone during the weekdays working and at weekends studying, he found the prospect of forced solitude disquieting. As he searched deeper and deeper within himself, his forced introspection eventually led back to memories of his childhood. With those memories came the prayers his parents had taught him and images of the temple in which his family had worshipped. As he meditated day after day, he felt himself being pulled towards the very subject for which he was being ostracised, pulled for the first time since leaving his parents' home back to the sanctity of Judaism.

Chapter 3

Early one morning after a heavy snowfall, Mr Wolff left his shop to spend an hour or two studying in the church. He was so isolated from the community now that he no longer cared what anyone thought of his continued historical research in the archives or delving into the peninsula's Jewish history. He crossed the square and noticed Karl near the foot of the hill. The boy looked up, saw him and ran to him. 'Where are you going?' Karl asked.

'To talk to God.'

Karl looked up at the church. It was Saturday morning. 'What about?'

'Come with me, if you like, but you'd better ask your mother first.'

Karl glanced at the shop to see if she was near the window. 'Will you wait for me?'

'I'll be in the vestry if you come.' Mr Wolff set off up the hill.

Karl watched him for a moment, then ran home. Ida told him to carry in the day's turf for the fire and he could go after that. When he reached the church he saw that the front door was ajar. He had never been into it alone before. He stood near the back pews and listened, then called Mr Wolff. His voice echoed round the walls, but the response was silence. Karl went back outside and looked around. Mr Wolff's footprints in the snow led into the building, but there were none to indicate that he had left. Karl went back inside and looked across the sanctuary to the vestry door. Through it, he could see the edge of a table. He walked up the aisle, glancing at the stained-glass window high above, went to the door and pushed it wide open. Mr Wolff was sitting at the table gazing at him.

'What are you doing?' Karl asked.

'I told you earlier.'

'Why aren't you out there?' Karl pointed to the pews where the villagers sat when they came up to the church alone to pray.

'I like it here. It's quieter.' He motioned for Karl to sit down at the other side of the table.

Karl glanced at the bookshelves lining the walls. He was impressed by Mr Wolff's knowledge of history and literature, and wanted to go to the most prestigious school, but only a small percentage of children were admitted to the Adolf Hitler Schools. He daydreamed of being the first in the village to be selected. To him, Mr Wolff was a model of academic excellence, and Mr Wolff knew of his ambition. He had likewise taken an interest in Karl, partly because his inquisitive nature reminded him of himself as a child.

Karl asked him more about the Knights who had built the church in which they now sat. 'Is it true that they fought a battle on this hill?'

'It's true,' he answered. 'This hill used to be a lookout for the ancient Prussians. After that battle the German Knights claimed the village for good. But even the ones who died conquering the village didn't much care.'

Mr Wolff explained that the highest goal a Knight could attain was not victory in battle, but death at the enemy's hands.

'They believed that by defencing the Virgin Mary's honour, they defended her son and in defending her son, they defended God.' Mr Wolff sometimes recited literary works for Karl; he said that they sometimes called themselves Mary's Knights or the cult of Mary and that in the fourteenth century they had created a vast body of Mary-verse, which they chanted in private among themselves:

> In the name of God's mother, the Virgin,
> Virtue's vessel and shedder of piercing tears,
> for the sake of avenging her only son, our Saviour,
> the renowned and numerous Knights of Mary
> chose death as their destiny and reward,
> and riddled with deep wounds
> kept open through fearlessness and Faith,
> they stood among smashed spears and shields,
> among godless corpses and limbs and heads
> to bleed and redeem with blood
> their rapturous hearts, their singing souls,
> in battles brutal as the Virgin is beautiful.

Around a month later Karl glanced out of his bedroom window and saw Mr Wolff walking up the path to the church again. When he had finished tidying his room, he left the house and followed him. He went in and crept round the wall until he reached the vestry door. There he stopped, certain that Mr Wolff was unaware of his presence. Then he scraped the heel of his boot on the floor. At first, Mr Wolff ignored it, but eventually he stood up to investigate.

When Mr Wolff pushed open the door to look out into the church, Karl hid behind it. He waited until Mr Wolff turned to go back, then jumped out and shouted, '*Achtung!*'

Mr Wolff whirled round in fright and Karl laughed until his sides ached.

When Mr Wolff had recovered he said, 'Come sit with me for a little while.'

They talked briefly about Karl's studies, then the coffin maker asked if Karl wanted to play a game.

'What kind of game?'

'You can pretend you're the Führer.'

At first Karl thought Mr Wolff was joking, but then he realised he was serious.

There was a moment's silence, before Mr Wolff asked, 'My dear Führer, how do you propose to run the country when the war is over?'

Without hesitating – he knew the Führer wouldn't hesitate – Karl said, 'We must continue helping our people – especially those living far away. We must make sure everyone is safe.'

'Everyone?'

Karl didn't understand the question, but answered confidently, as he knew a leader must, 'Yes, of course.'

They continued their dialogue, until Mr Wolff ended it by telling him he would make a fine leader. Karl swelled with pride. Unlike many people he knew, Mr Wolff never paid a compliment unless he meant it.

That meeting made a deep impression on Karl. Even though he and the coffin maker had spent only a short time together, he knew the old man had taught him something important even if he couldn't quite put his finger on what it was. When he left the church, he decided he wanted to be alone to think about their conversation. Instead of continuing towards the square, he went down the hill into the forest where the hidden tunnel was rumoured to open.

Chapter 4

In the months that followed, Karl was so busy at school that he hardly saw Mr Wolff – until one afternoon, when he glanced out his bedroom window: strangers were talking to him outside his shop and examining his identity card. He had shown it to Karl one morning when they met on the road that led from the railway station. Mr Wolff had been to the capital. Karl had studied the card, which bore a large 'J' imprinted in the middle.

'They want me to change my name to Israel now,' Mr Wolff had said. 'Israel and Sara.'

After the men had left, Mr Wolff remained outside his shop for a long time, staring across the square. When he finally turned to go in, he saw Karl and paused, briefly, before disappearing back inside. Karl felt uneasy about having spied on him in such an uncomfortable situation.

But he felt far worse when, on his return from school a few weeks later, he discovered that Mr Wolff had gone. When Karl asked his mother what had happened she didn't answer. A few hours later he asked her again. She told him to mind his own business. Later still, when she found him in his room, looking out of the window at Mr Wolff's shop, she relented. He knew something was wrong because she avoided his eyes.

'They took Mr Schultze, too,' she said.

'Where did they go?'

'I don't know. They put them in a truck.'

'Are they coming back?'

'I don't know.'

'What about his shop?'

'I told you, I don't know!'

He knew he should not ask any more. They stared out of the window without speaking. Ida slid her hand along Karl's arm and clasped his hand in hers. He continued to look out of the window, first at the linden tree in the centre of the square, then at the church where he and Mr Wolff had sat together. Eventually, Karl asked if he could go outside.

'I want you to stay in,' his mother said softly. 'They might come back to do something to his shop.'

In the months after Mr Wolff's disappearance, the children ran up the hill to the churchyard each day when their parents let them out to play. Once, Karl led the others into the church and up the stone stairs to the turret. Halfway up they came to a door that had been sealed with bricks. Karl placed his palms on the bricks, as Mr Wolff once had, and said, 'The secret tunnel is in here.' He explained that behind the bricks another stairway led down into the earth. 'The tunnel may have caved in by now,' he added and told them that the other end had also been sealed. No one in the village was sure any longer exactly where it came out.

When they left the church the children stopped and turned back to look at where they imagined the hidden stairs led down into the earth. A noise from the rooftop distracted them. They looked up and saw balanced carefully on the peak a stork's nest made from twigs with a large bird in it. Atop the ridgeline of each house in the village ran a single strand of taut wire affixed to two boards secured at opposite ends of the roof to prevent the heavy birds from landing and keeping the home owners awake at night as they created a racket building nests. Suddenly the stork took flight and swooped down towards them. The children scattered in all directions.

Chapter 5

In the early spring of 1941, while the last of the snow still lay on the ground, Karl, Peter and Leyna were building a snowman when they saw someone walking towards the village on the road leading from Fischhausen. The children stopped to watch the stranger approach. He was carrying a parcel under his arm. Leyna waved. Karl pushed her hand down: 'Don't wave at strangers, stupid.'

A moment later Karl recognised the man. He paused to make sure he wasn't wrong and took off towards him, Peter and Leyna following.

'Father!' Karl grabbed his hand.

'You're too old to behave like a child,' his father said, with no trace of a smile.

Karl paused before asking, 'Did you bring some chocolate?'

By then all three children were standing in front of their father. When Leyna held out her arms, he smiled for the first time, bent down and picked her up. 'Have you boys been helping your mother?' he asked and kissed Leyna's cheek.

'We do everything,' Karl said.

'We even tidy our rooms,' Peter added.

Their father's face didn't reflect their own excitement, but Karl and Peter could hardly contain themselves. Both ran for home, wanting to be the first to tell their mother that their father was here.

Ida was in the kitchen preparing a goose for delivery to a family in Bersnicken, the next village north of Germau – they were expecting their son home from Berlin: he had been sent to the capital after his promotion to Scharführer of his Hitler Youth unit. Although the shop was closed, Ida continued to make a little money dressing poultry. When she heard the boys come in noisily and run for the kitchen without taking off their boots, she marched to the kitchen door and yelled, 'Go back and take—' She broke off as she saw Paul through the living-room window with Leyna in his arms.

She went back to the sink, dropped the knife, rinsed her hands under the tap and began to cry. Her husband came in for the first time in almost two years.

Once she had controlled herself she turned round. Paul walked to the middle of the kitchen, but did not reach her. She stepped forward and put out her arms to embrace him. He stepped back before she was able to slide her arms round him.

For a few seconds she stood in front of her husband. Although there was only half a metre between them, it was as though she were utterly alone, as she had been since his departure for Paris. Tears filled her eyes again and at last seemed to provide Paul with an unspoken cue, for he relented. He moved forward, took her in his arms and held her tightly.

Throughout the morning, as word spread, people called at the shop to welcome him home. After Mr Laufer had insisted on a celebratory drink, Ida pulled Paul into the kitchen. 'Please, not today. I haven't seen you for so long. We must spend at least a day alone as a family.'

'It's only a toast. Surely you don't want me to offend him?' They heard another knock.

'More drinks?'

'What do you expect me to do? Tell them to go home? Some are customers. The war will end soon and we'll need them to come back to us.'

'Then let's go to the coast. We can celebrate when we get back. We'll have two or three days alone. Tell your friends to organise a party here at the shop.'

It was soon settled. Someone offered to lend his horse and wagon for their trip. 'Could you take us to the station instead?' Paul asked.

It was nearly dusk when they reached Sarkau. There was only one inn. A sign informed travellers that it was closed. Paul knocked anyway. A woman opened the door and pointed to the sign. 'Can't you read?'

'I'm here with my family. We have nowhere else to go.'

'We're closed.' She began to shut the door.

'I've just returned from Paris,' Paul said. 'We need a room for two nights.' He knew she wouldn't refuse a soldier.

'Very well. We're expecting family at the end of the week.' She opened the door and pointed up the stairs. 'The two rooms at the top on the right.'

The following morning the family followed a snowy pathway through the pine forest towards the sea. Halfway there they climbed a small rise and a series of dunes came into view. Covered with snow, they looked like giant cumulus clouds turned upside-down and tethered to the ground. Beyond, waves lapped the shore. Karl ran ahead, climbing to the top of the highest dune, Peter behind him, trying to keep up with his brother. Surrounded by dunes, with the water stretching as far as he could see, Karl felt as though he had reached the end of the earth.

Later, as they walked back through the forest to the inn, Paul asked Ida why she had been so quiet all afternoon: 'You hardly said a word on the train.'

'I don't like the games you're playing.'

'What are you talking about?'

'You come home and can't bring yourself to kiss me.'

'You're not the only one who's hurting.'

'I'm scared,' she said.

'Of what?'

'I don't know . . . of what's going to happen. It doesn't seem like the war will lead to anything great.'

'It won't last for ever. I'll be home for good soon.'

'That's what you said when you went to Paris.'

'Well, you don't seem to want me here anyway.'

Ida didn't answer. Paul slid his hand round her waist. This time it was Ida who pulled away, but when he persisted she laid her hand on his and their fingers interlocked.

On the morning of their departure for Germau the family walked silently to the road to flag down a vehicle going to Cranz to catch the train home. Ever since Paul could remember, the spit protruding from the northern shore of the peninsula had been a national park, closed to traffic, but while he had been in Paris a new road had been built through the middle for the heavy military traffic that went back and forth to Memel. Three trucks passed them without stopping. When the fourth approached, Paul stepped into the road. The driver and he exchanged a few words, then they all climbed into the cramped cab. Inside the air was stuffy and too warm. Ida rolled down the window a crack.

The driver was young, a boy almost, from Hesse. He soon became talkative, attempting to impress the higher-ranked Paul. He spoke with an accent Ida and the children found odd, but his words were clear enough.

'It's my first time in East Prussia. I never realised how far from home it is.'

'Were you in France?' Paul asked.

'No, I was sent straight here.'

Karl and Peter sat quietly between the driver and their parents. Paul held Leyna on his lap. Ida watched the military trucks going north through the pine forest, which had been planted on the wide sandy spit in the late nineteenth century to prevent it from being washed away by the sea.

The family returned home for the party in Paul's honour. Talk focused on everyone's plans for after the war. The mood was subdued. Most of the older men seemed certain the war would soon be over, but Paul wouldn't be drawn.

On the morning of his departure the children followed him and Ida as they walked to the station. The next day Paul was due at a base in Poland. He didn't know when or if he would be permitted another leave. On the platform, he kissed Ida and the children. He was preoccupied, as if his military duties were more important now than his family, but he had always been like that when he was thinking about work. Now, though, he wasn't just going to work in the shop behind their home, he was leaving for a month, a year, two years? No one knew.

His father's indifference that morning stuck in Karl's mind. The train pulled away, clanking along the tracks. Ida and the children were left alone on the platform to watch it disappear from view. They remained staring down the narrowing tracks long after the train vanished, as an uncanny calmness similar to the silence that follows the first heavy snow each year enveloped the family. Leyna tugged at her mother's hand. Their sister's movement caused the boys to glance up at their mother. 'I want to go home,' she said.

They walked down the steps from the platform, across the steel tracks slick with ice and to the path in the field. There, they fell into single file. A light snow began to fall. Karl, at the back, stopped to look up. The uniform sky provided nothing against which to distinguish itself as a sheet of ashen grey slowly descended over them. He tried to separate a single cloud from the mass so he could imagine the snow falling from that particular place, but the sky offered no depth of field, refusing to cooperate with Karl's wish for something to recognise. The snowfall grew heavier, causing even the backdrop of the pallid sky to disappear in a white flurry.

Ida stopped to adjust her hat, leaned down and picked up Leyna.

When they reached the road, the cobbles were buried under a thin layer of fresh snow, which highlighted the imperfections in the road's surface.

Tirskone, an elderly man from Powayen, the village nearest the station, often walked along the road with a shovel and a bucket of sand with which he smoothed the ground beneath an uneven cobble or poured sand into an empty hole before he inserted a new one. He kept stacks of stones in the brush at intervals along the roadside. Each year a government truck came from Königsberg and left a pile that Tirskone would move, five at a time, to his hiding places. Once Karl had crouched in the bushes to watch him.

Tirskone, like Paul, rarely spoke. When he did it was to make a request, delivered as an order, for a drink of water while he repaired the cobbles in the square. Now Karl glanced up and down the road, expecting to see the old man's footprints: light snow rarely kept Tirskone indoors.

'Let's take the road this time. I don't want to walk back through the forest while it's snowing,' Ida said.

Karl's eyes were on the low hill that led into Germau less than a kilometre away. 'Can I take the path?' he asked.

'Don't be long.'

Ida glanced at Peter, shivering beside her. 'You can come with me,' she said. 'You can play with your brother later.'

Karl followed the path into the forest to the brook below the church, imagining what the ancient Balt-Prussian tribe would do if they saw the Teutonic Knights escaping from their secret tunnel. He imagined some clan members pulling out their swords as they whispered among themselves in the undergrowth. Karl kicked up branches in the snow, until he found one that fitted his hands, so he could join the tribe slaying the invaders. He swung it to get a feel for its weight before sticking its tip into the snow beside him while glancing up the hill at the large church and caught his breath.

He decided to sneak up behind the church – it would be easier to surprise the enemy if he went that way. Crouching, he stalked through the woods. As the hill steepened, he picked up speed. When he reached a point from which he could approach the church directly, he broke into a run, crested the summit and darted out past the cemetery. At the corner, he raised his sword, jumped out in front of the church and swung wildly at a group of Knights. He thrust, parried and turned about until his arms ached, then plopped down into the snow, dizzy.

The clearing was empty. Nobody had walked up the hill that morning so the snow lay undisturbed. He could have killed a couple more, he thought, if he had come up the opposite side. He didn't like playing this game with the other village children: they were younger and he could run faster so it was too easy to kill them. He remembered the youth group he would soon join – maybe he could play it with them. Most of the boys already in the group were from other villages and he knew they'd want to see the entrance to the secret tunnel in his church.

He stood up and walked across the field to a low wall a short distance above the square and looked away from the village towards Willkau, then looked back at the houses below. His mother stepped out of the shop door and called him.

'Coming,' he shouted.

She looked up at the wall. 'I told you not to be long. Come here – you haven't finished the jobs I asked you to do,' she shouted.

He ran down the path, hoping she wasn't angry. Even when she was, though, she was not like his father could be. While he would never admit it to her, he was relieved his father had gone again – even to the dangers of war.

Chapter 6

At the beginning of June, Ida received a short letter from Paul to say that he had been transferred east of Warsaw. He had included a photograph of himself sitting on the motorcycle that he rode to check the food supplies for the hospital he was supervising. 'I'm not sure when you'll hear from me again. There's hardly enough time to sleep, much less to write letters,' he concluded.

On the twenty-second, Ida was in the kitchen getting breakfast for the children with the radio on. As she leaned down to take a tray out of the oven, an announcer interrupted the music to introduce Joseph Goebbels, who said he had an urgent message from the Führer: 'Weighed down with emotion, condemned to months of silence, I can finally speak freely to you, the German people. At this moment a march is taking place that, in its extent, compares with the greatest the world has ever seen. I have decided again today to place the fate and future of the empire and our people in the hands of our soldiers. May God help us . . .' Before sunrise, Goebbels said, the army had launched an attack on Russia.

Ida thought of Paul on his motorcycle moving slowly alongside a column. The image frightened her, so instead she imagined him in a jeep behind the front line, and then at his desk in the office at the hospital. It was safer there, she told herself. She reminded herself of his arrival in Paris the day after it fell: he had avoided combat then, so why not now? Their love had cooled, but Ida wanted her children's father to live. She tried to convince herself that when he finally returned for good he would be kinder to her and the children.

When Karl came downstairs half an hour later, she tried to think of a way to explain what had happened, but she didn't understand why Germany was attacking Russia. She had understood the offensive against the French – during her childhood her father had talked incessantly about the injustices of the Treaty of Versailles – but she could think of no reason to justify their attack on Russia, especially since Russia in the Non-Aggression Pact had agreed not to attack Germany.

At breakfast, Karl noticed his mother distressed and anxious, but she said nothing and he didn't ask; he had to meet a boy from a neighbouring village to go to a youth group meeting. When they arrived, he soon learned what had upset his mother: the attack was on everybody's lips. One boy said his father was killing Russians at that very moment.

'I thought he was an army cook. The only way he'll ever kill someone is with food poisoning.'

A boy from Warschken, another village nearby, turned to Karl and said, 'Maybe your father will send sweets from Moscow.'

'Maybe he won't go there,' Karl replied.

'Of course he will. The whole army's going.'

They were convinced that the German army would beat the Russians, and anyone whose father or grandfather had fought at the battle of Tannenberg compared it with what was happening now. No one had grasped that the present offensive, three or four hundred kilometres to the east, was not just a battle but the start of a new war: the Soviet-German War.

Three million German soldiers were pitted against the same number of Russians, whose opposing army would soon grow to six million. The largest military invasion ever was under way. Across eastern Europe the boys' fathers were behind thousands of heavy guns, pounding Russian positions. Soon the front would extend over four thousand kilometres, from the Baltic Sea in the north to the Black Sea in the south, the entire land mass of eastern Europe sealed behind a wall of German soldiers and guns.

One boy announced that Hitler himself was in East Prussia, unaware that the Führer had constructed new headquarters there from which to direct the offensive. The Wolfsschanze – Wolf's Lair – was buried deep in the forests south-east of Samland.

Before the offensive had begun, the Prussian army commanders – a constant source of irritation to Hitler – were far from united behind the decision to invade Russia. Some had agreed that if they had to go ahead, now was the best time to surprise the enemy because Stalin had murdered his best commanders during the Great Purge of 1936 to 1938. Others, though, would have preferred to abide by the Non-Aggression Pact: the steppes were too vast and the war was being fought on too many other fronts. Hitler himself had once written that an attack on Russia, as well as a western theatre, would spell the end of Germany.

BOOK II

A Childhood

Chapter 1

Once the war with Russia was under way Germau remained oddly calm. For a time photographs were published in Königsberg newspapers showing Latvians, Lithuanians and Ukrainians welcoming German soldiers as liberators freeing them from Stalin's tyranny. Ida's sister, in Berlin, rarely mentioned the war in her letters.

That spring, shortly before the Führer's birthday, a Hitler Youth representative had come to the village to talk to Ida about a ceremony that Karl was to attend. Ida was reluctant to let him go, but she had no choice. Karl by contrast was more excited than she had ever seen him. He had gone with the man and a large group of boys from the peninsula by train to Pillau where they crossed the Bay of Danzig on a Strength Through Joy cruise liner.

Two older boys had stolen some photographs of Jewish prisoners, which they wanted to get rid of now – they knew they would get into trouble if the theft was discovered. They had concealed the evidence among the younger boys' belongings. When Karl found three photos in his clothes, he became frightened and pushed them to the bottom of his bag. He would throw them away when he got home.

From Danzig, the younger boys went on to Marienburg, the

ancient headquarters of the Teutonic Knights with the largest castle Karl had ever seen. They arrived at dusk and joined thousands of others. Karl's group entered a huge chamber illuminated by torchlight. They stood to attention for nearly two hours as they sang Hitler Youth songs and listened to a long speech: the Reichsjugendführer, the highest-ranking official in the league, talked endlessly about commitment, discipline and personal strength. Later, each new recruit took an oath under the flickering torches: 'I promise that, in the Hitler Youth, I will always do my duty, with love and faithfulness, and help the Führer, so help me God.'

Afterwards the hall reverberated to the boom of drums, the boys' faces glowing orange in the torchlight. Soon they were singing again – a thousand boys in harmony – 'Forward, forward . . .' The sounds echoed in Karl's mind long after he had returned to Germau.

In July he went camping with his group to Palmnicken where they pitched tents on a plateau above the Baltic. On the first night after the leader had told everyone to go to sleep, Karl felt the hand of the boy to his left slide across his belly and downwards. Startled, he pretended to be asleep. Soon he felt a new and pleasant sensation, one he'd never experienced before, between his legs. He turned over – and the boy on his right kissed him on his mouth. Karl tensed, and the first boy whispered that he would report him if he didn't join in with their game.

The next morning, the three behaved as if nothing had happened. Karl climbed out of the tent and walked over to where the ground fell away to the sea below and watched two men in a pit carrying a burlap sack filled with amber. When he turned back to see the other boys coming out of their tents, he wondered if they were harbouring a similar secret.

That afternoon the leader took the boys through the woods and across a field, beyond which the blue-green waters of the Baltic stretched to the horizon. At points along the western edge of the peninsula, steep sandy cliffs fell as much as ten metres to the beach below. The leader announced that to earn a dagger, each boy must run at top speed to the edge of the cliff and jump out as far as he could.

'What if we're killed?' a boy asked.

'I'll give the knife to your mother.'

Laughter erupted.

'It's only sand, idiot,' a boy near the back yelled.

'But my cousin broke his leg falling from the cliff in Rauschen.'

The leader told them that each boy would run and jump, then get up, move out of the way and remain on the beach with the assistant, who was already down there. 'If you do break your leg don't scream. You don't want to be captured by the Russians, do you?'

He pointed at a terrified-looking boy. 'You first. Run on the count of three.'

'But—'

'One. Two—'

The boy started running.

'I said on the count of three!' shouted the leader. 'Faster!'

The boy's pace increased and the group held their breath when he neared the edge of the cliff, expecting him to stop. But he didn't hesitate. He ran forward, his eyes on the horizon, until the ground fell from beneath his feet and he disappeared. They heard him scream, and the distant roar of breakers.

The sixteen-year-old leader walked back to them grinning. 'Let's hope he's not dead.'

This time nobody laughed.

'Anyone scared?'

The group were mute.

'I'm going to stand here and watch until every one of you has jumped off the cliff. Anyone who slows down before he jumps doesn't get his dagger.'

As Karl waited, he looked over the tall grass to the cliff's edge, feeling as if he had been called to a duty greater than himself. That spring the leader had come to his village only for him: no other local children had gone to the castle at Marienburg. He felt an epiphany of quietness as he prepared for his jump – and dismissed the fleeting thought that last night's illicit adventure might have contributed to today's confidence. He pictured himself walking into Germau with his shoulder strap across his chest and his new dagger on his belt.

When the leader signalled to him, he started to run and felt himself stride, with a sense of supreme confidence. As he neared the edge of the cliff, his eyes rose above the horizon – he leapt as high as possible, aware that his body sailing into the sky towards the sea created a silhouette seen by the leader and boys who still waited their turn. Airborne, he squeezed his eyes shut. He wanted to remember for ever how it felt to float over the earth, the air above coalescing with the water below, whose merging currents buoyed him as he floated outwards into its transmuting body.

Chapter 2

When he got home two days later, Karl didn't tell his mother what had happened in the tent, but he showed her his new knife. She wasn't very interested; he decided she hadn't grasped its significance. However, he would always have been the first in his village to join the youth group, which no one in Germau would forget. The children were already asking him about his adventures.

Ida took the dagger from him and read the inscription, 'Blood and Honour', then handed it back. 'We have enough knives. I wish they'd given you something useful.'

'It *is* useful.'

Ida didn't argue. 'It's time for your piano practice.'

'But I told everyone I'd go back out after I'd shown you the knife.'

'All right then, just for a little while. But I want you to practise before supper.'

When Karl opened the front door the children had gathered round the tree at the centre of the square, waiting for him.

'Can I hold it?' Salomo asked.

'In a minute.'

The children followed Karl up past the church to the field beside the cemetery, where he pulled the dagger from its sheath

37

and sat down in the grass. 'Don't cut yourself,' he said, as he held it out to Salomo. The knife went round the circle. Even the girls were fascinated.

'Did they make you kill anyone?' Salomo asked.

Karl looked at him with contempt. 'You're such an idiot. Why would we kill anyone?'

'I'm just asking.'

'They made us jump off a cliff, though.'

'Did anyone die?'

Karl ignored him. After he had put the dagger back into its sheath, he suggested they play Search and Destroy. They stood up and milled about for a while, deciding on the names of the units they would pretend to be in. Karl told them the best was called Das Reich. 'You can do anything you want in it,' he said. 'Not even the regular army can tell you what to do.' He had heard that the élite SS unit couldn't get into trouble for anything – even killing people.

Paula, who would be ten next spring, said, 'The Jungmädel is better than Das Reich.'

The boys laughed: the girls' youth group better than Das Reich? Ridiculous!

Karl tried to imagine Paula riding on a tank as he chose sides for the game. Suddenly the girls realised he was only picking the boys.

'We're playing, too,' Paula demanded.

'Fetch us some food if you want to join in,' one of the boys shouted.

'And don't forget to wash the dishes,' Peter added.

Any semblance of order broke down as the girls ran at the boys, who raced off in all directions across the field. When Peter caught a girl at the far end of the field near the woods he said, 'Pull your pants down and maybe we'll let you play.'

'You first,' she said.

'The leader doesn't go first.'

'Then I shan't.'

For no apparent reason, Peter threw up his arm and shouted, '*Sieg Heil!*'

The boys on the other side of the field stopped and looked at him and the girl.

'Don't waste it on a girl!' Karl screamed.

Over the following year the children carried on playing new games, imitating the stories that the older youth group members shared. The games acquired a distinctly militaristic element, the children both inventive and dogmatic. But no matter how disciplined they pretended to be, the games always broke down by the time the play day ended, order giving way to chaos, discipline disintegrating into confusion.

Karl and Peter did not hear from their father for six months. When a note did finally arrive in December 1942, he told them he was in Russia, but didn't say where. 'We're busy,' he wrote. 'Always busy.' Something in the tone, or perhaps the note's brevity, made him sound even more distant.

Ida tried not to worry about the lack of communication between herself and her husband. He was so far away and, after all, the country was at war: she shouldn't expect any more. She tried to forget that an acquaintance received a letter every month from her husband in Russia. Ida had stopped visiting her: the only thing the woman talked about was her latest letter from her husband.

Rumours were spreading that the troops in Stalingrad were failing against the Russians, but Ida had heard no such news over the radio. Hitler continued to broadcast to German women, desperate to hold their loyalty. Many, like Ida's sister, felt a strong bond with him that had developed from the broadcasts and were sure that he would tell them if the situation changed. Ida worried that the radio news neither confirmed nor denied what they all heard from injured soldiers returning home.

Karl continued attending school in Pillau near the military base that sprawled through much of the port town. He had been top of the class in the three Latin tests that year. His teacher had told him that he would recommend him for the Adolf Hitler School. Karl knew that if he won a place, he had a strong chance of one day reaching a high position in the government. Early in 1943 Hitler Youth received the annual slogan. It hung above the blackboard in the mathematics room: 'War Service for German Youth'.

That winter the only thing he didn't like about going to school in Pillau was coming home by train after dark, especially during a new moon. He dreaded the moment when the train dropped him off on the empty platform two kilometres from his house. The forest was so dark when he walked alone back to the village and he always felt as if something or someone were watching him among the trees. He would walk in the middle of the road so that nothing could reach him from the edge, feeling his way through the darkness between tree cover and the clouds, the lack of light sometimes making him feel as though he had been locked inside a giant room from which he had to find his way out. Whenever his feet touched the dirt at the edge of the road, he would sprint back to the middle. Over time he developed the ability to steer down the middle as he slowly became accustomed to his temporary blindness. When he reached the rise that led over the small climb before dropping into Germau, he increased his pace. Every night was the same: he never felt safe until he reached the top of the small hill and saw the shimmering lights below surrounding the square.

Chapter 3

By the autumn of 1943 little of the news that filtered into the peninsula villages was good. During the summer the Russians had started a counter-offensive and wounded soldiers occasionally came home on leave. A young man from Sacherau had lost his hand, but planned to return to the front as soon as the wound healed. He told the children how retreating German troops destroyed everything they came across. He was part of an SS demolition squad and had blown off his hand as his regiment pulled back across the Ukraine towards Poland. He said they had set entire villages ablaze and used flame-throwers to scorch wheatfields so that the Russian divisions had no shelter or food as they pushed across the steppes towards Germany. He was confident that they would be stopped by the time they reached Poland and he wanted to be there for the celebration when the Russians had been defeated.

In Berlin the constant bombing had forced Ida's sister Elsa to send her son to his aunt: on the peninsula there was still little sign of war, except for a rare troop transport passing through the square on its way between Memel and Pillau. Elsa remained in Berlin: she had secured a coveted job at the Chancellery.

Ida felt certain that Karl and Peter especially would be

delighted to see Otto and sent them down to Pillau to pick him up. She thought they'd find it easier to get to know each other without her presence. As soon as they had gone, she began to prepare the evening meal – she had invited her father and step-mother, too. The boys returned earlier than she had expected, so after she had kissed Otto she gave them each a basket and dispatched them to the forest for mushrooms.

As always, Karl took it upon himself to act as their leader. An only child, Otto wasn't used to taking orders from someone of around his own age, but he soon realised that he would have to if he didn't want to get lost. Like the children in the village, Otto was fascinated by Karl's knife. He knew many boys in Berlin who had joined the Hitler Youth, but none had offered to let him examine theirs. Karl told him about the camping trips and his leap from the cliff. Peter then suggested they show Otto the photographs. When Karl had returned from Marienburg he hadn't thrown them away. Instead, he had told his brother to hide them in an abandoned shed near a local farm. Now he thought again for a moment, then told Otto he could look at them, provided he didn't tell anyone.

When they reached the shed, Peter went in, pulled up a decaying floorboard and got them out of the box he had hidden beneath it.

The first showed a group of men huddled together for warmth. In the second photograph four women were standing in what looked like dormitories. One of the women didn't have a shirt on, her breasts fully exposed to the camera. The last was of a girl with a boy, perhaps her older brother, and a woman who appeared to be their mother. Whenever Peter came to the shed alone, this was the one he looked at most often.

'Jews?' Otto asked.

His question unsettled the brothers. They had been staring at the girl, who seemed to stare back.

'Who else?' Karl snapped.

In an attempt to absolve himself, Karl explained how some older boys had stolen them and hidden them among his possessions.

'Does everyone have photos like these?' Otto asked.

'Of course not! Why do you think they had to get rid of them? No one knows I've got them except you and Peter, and if you tell anyone about them I'll say you brought them from Berlin.'

'I said I wouldn't tell.'

Peter returned the photos to their hiding place and the boys went back to the main road, making sure nobody saw them as they emerged from the bushes. The woodland where Ida and the children found mushrooms was a few kilometres further on. Karl and Peter knew all the varieties, including the poisonous ones. Amanitas grew everywhere on the peninsula and Ida had warned them that a single cap could kill an entire family. The first time Karl saw one his mother had said, 'Nature made them bright red so you'll notice them and eat one. Then your body will fertilise the ground so that more can grow.' She then had picked a few caps, which she placed in a separate cloth to take home. That afternoon, she filled an old pan with water and boiled them, let the liquid cool, then placed it inside the door of the slaughterhouse where it enticed flies to land, drink and die. 'It's nature's way of controlling pests too,' she had added.

Along the road to the forest, Karl told Otto not to touch the bright-red mushrooms with white spots: 'They'll kill you.'

Otto wondered about these woods: the only woods he had ever been in were in the Tiergarten near the centre of Berlin, and Grunewald, at the edge of the city, where he had always felt safe, because other people were invariably around. Germau seemed to be in the middle of nowhere.

When they reached the edge of the forest, Karl pointed out the path. 'Follow us and you won't get lost, but if you get separated just yell. We won't be far.'

As soon as they were among the trees Karl and Peter were finding and picking mushrooms. Otto stayed with them, but instead of looking for mushrooms he was remembering the stories his mother had read to him about children leaving peas or breadcrumbs along their path so that they could find their way out. Once in a while he would hear a rustle and rush to tell his cousins, but they laughed at his fears. Karl led them off the path into a darker area where the trees grew so close together that almost no light reached the forest floor. 'Mushrooms grow better in the dark,' he said. 'We'll find plenty here.'

Suddenly the ground had become too wet to walk across, so Karl set off in a wide arc round the bog. Then, as they were pushing through a thicket, they heard a shrill scream. They stopped in their tracks. The sound faded, then came again.

'Is it an animal?' Otto whispered.

'Maybe something's stuck in a trap,' Peter suggested.

'It's coming from the direction of Lengniethen,' Karl decided.

It was a lonely place, but the local trapper, Ludwig Schneider, lived there with his family. The boys followed the sound until they came to a little glade. Karl held up a hand to stop the others, as Peter saw something move on the other side of the clearing. He stepped close to his brother and pointed silently.

The boys crept forward, then stopped again. Through the brush on the other side of the clearing they glimpsed a man, but they were still too far away to discern who he was and what was going on. They fell to the ground and crawled nearer.

It was Ludwig, Karl realised. He was with Uta – she had gone to primary school in Germau until Ludwig had hired her to help his wife. Now she was leaning against a tree and Ludwig had pulled up her dress as if he were about to spank her. But he was standing too close to her for that and moving in a peculiar way. Then the boys heard that sound again. Was Uta crying? When Ludwig grabbed her hair she stopped.

Terror gripped the boys. They didn't know whether to run into the field so that Ludwig would see them and be distracted, or race home and tell their mother what was going on. Karl and Peter knew they had to be careful – Ludwig was said to have killed a man for hunting in his territory. It was best to say nothing, Karl decided, and began to inch backwards. He gestured to the others that they should follow and laid a finger over his lips. Once they were back among the trees, each boy grabbed his basket and fled. They didn't stop for more mushrooms but hurried on until they reached the road. Back in the open, they walked quickly towards the village and agreed not to tell anyone what they had seen.

When they went into the kitchen Ida saw straight away that something was wrong: only a thin layer of mushrooms covered the bottom of the baskets. 'Have you boys been in trouble?'

'Otto wanted to come home and see if Grandpa had arrived.'

Ida looked at her elder son sceptically. 'I told you he'd be here at suppertime. Go back and find some more mushrooms.'

'But there aren't any more.'

'Nonsense! There are so many you couldn't carry them all. It'll be cold in a few weeks and then there won't be any. Don't come back again until those baskets are full.'

The boys turned to go.

'Leave the ones you've already got and I'll clean them.'

The boys did as they were told, but before they went out, Karl saw Leyna sitting on the floor in the living room, playing with her teddy bear. He went in and kicked it out of her hands and across the room. It came to rest under the piano stool and Leyna began to cry. He ran to retrieve it and shoved it back into her hands.

'What's going on?' Ida called from the kitchen.

'Nothing,' Karl shouted.

'Leave Leyna alone.'

They slipped out of the front door before Ida had had time to investigate.

'Let's go up past the church,' Karl suggested.

'There're no mushrooms up there,' his brother reminded him.

'We'll try the woods on the other side.'

This time they ignored the path. Karl and Peter knew that any mushrooms that grew beside it would have been picked already. None of the older women ventured far from the path: just a few decades earlier, wolves and bears had patrolled these woods. The boys knew that if they went a little way along the brook and pushed their way through a series of thickets, they would find mushrooms sprouting everywhere.

Soon they were picking furiously to see who could fill his basket first in an effort to forget what they had seen earlier. At first, Otto lagged behind the others, but when he forced himself to concentrate on what he was doing, and put the disturbing images out of his mind, he began to catch up. When he had filled his basket, his cousins were still loading theirs.

Karl didn't like to be beaten, so when Otto appeared with a full basket he ignored him and went on piling mushrooms into his own.

Even though Otto had agreed that he would not mention to Ida what they had witnessed in the forest, he felt uneasy. He had seen people kissing in the Tiergarten and even a girl's shirt unbuttoned, but nothing like what that man had been doing to Uta. He wondered for a moment if people were different in the country, then thought better of it: even Karl had seemed upset by what they had seen.

When they got back to the shop, Landwirt was sitting on the steps with Leyna in his arms. Otto had met his grandfather just three times before, twice when the old man had come to Berlin and once when Otto and Elsa had gone to Königsberg for his grandmother's funeral. His grandfather was almost a stranger to him. Otto greeted him somewhat formally, then Landwirt asked after his daughter Elsa.

While Otto answered him, Karl glanced at the door to the shop to make sure his mother wasn't within earshot. Then, when his cousin fell silent, he said, 'Can we have a drink, Grandpa? It's Otto's first day after all.'

Landwirt laughed. 'I put a little bottle of Bärenfang behind the turf stack,' he whispered. 'Don't get drunk – and don't tell your mother I gave it to you when you do!'

Chapter 4

In late spring, although all civilians had been ordered over the radio to remain at home, refugees occasionally arrived in the village – but sometimes a week went by without one appearing on the square, in search of the road to Pillau. Unfortunately, few civilian ships were sailing, so their best chance of moving west was to return to Königsberg and follow Reichsstrasse 1, which connected the city with Berlin.

Near midnight on 20 July, Ida sat alone in the living room, sewing as she listened to the radio. Suddenly the programme was interrupted by the Führer. That morning an army commander had placed a bomb in his meeting room, he said. It had exploded, killing a secretary, but he himself had escaped virtually unharmed.

By now, many officers who had once supported him no longer trusted his leadership: he had destroyed Germany's much admired General Staff system by demanding to see almost every major order and strategic plan, then revising it before sending it on, without recourse to trained officers. Also, he placed his favourites in high-ranking posts they were ill equipped to fulfil. Now, although the army was still winning minor battles, it was losing ground. The officers who were conspiring to kill him had no intention of surrendering to the enemy when he had gone, but planned to reassert Germany's military supremacy.

As Ida listened to the Führer's angry voice, she realised for the first time that her own family might be in danger if the war did not soon turn back in Germany's favour. She knew the history of the peninsula almost as well as her father did. No one had occupied it successfully since the French in June 1807 and it had been nearly fifty years before that when the Russians had carried out their only successful occupation of the peninsula during the Seven Years War.

Early the next morning when Karl came downstairs, he found his mother asleep on the davenport. On the radio a woman was singing about summer. He went to Ida, wondering if he should wake her, but before he reached her she opened her eyes.

'Were you up all night?' he asked.

'Come here,' she said, patting the seat beside her.

Karl sat down and she kissed him. 'I must have fallen asleep while I was sewing. Why are you up so early?'

'I heard the radio. I thought you were listening to the records Father brought from Paris.'

'I haven't put them on since he left.'

His father had bought the radiogram before the war when they had a contract to deliver meat to the nearby military base, Karl remembered. Before Paul's departure for France, the neighbours had come to listen to it.

'Would you like to play a record?' Ida asked.

'Now?'

'Why not? Do you know how to put it on?'

Karl jumped up and grabbed his favourite from beneath the sofa, where the records were kept. Perfectly circular and flat, he loved its feel and solid, heavy weight. He knew it would shatter if dropped, so he carried it carefully across the room. Ida knew which one he had chosen. It was the only one he ever listened to – a Hot Club de France recording, with Django Reinhardt, the guitarist, and Stéphane Grappelli on violin. Ever since Paul had bought it, Karl had begged her for a guitar. She had told him that if he learned to play the piano well enough, she'd consider it after the war. The piece Karl liked best was 'Nuages', and now, as the unusual chord sequence that opened it filled the room, he came back to sit beside his mother. She held out her arms and Karl snuggled into her as Reinhardt played.

Chapter 5

While Otto enjoyed running around with his cousins, he didn't like Karl. It was partly to do with the way Karl flaunted his dagger and belt, the only ones in the village, but mostly because Karl ordered him about. Sometimes he ignored him, even if it meant being beaten up – which was how Karl kept his brother in line.

When there were no household tasks to be done, no school or youth group meeting to attend, they went hiking. They'd climb the hill to the church, drop into the forest and follow the path until it petered out, then continue through virgin woodland. They called it their survival game. When they moved south-east they bypassed Krattlau and Anchenthal, which were little more than clusters of houses at a crossroads. They avoided two lone houses at another crossroads and scouted through the forest to Ellerhaus, another hamlet, where they came out to knock on a door and ask for a drink of water.

A man named Volker was working in his field when the boys came into the village. He grinned when he saw them. 'What are you up to?'

'Hiking,' Karl answered. 'Otto here is still learning. He's our cousin but he's lived in the city all his life.'

'How do you like Samland?'

'It's easy to get lost,' Otto said.

'Trust your senses.'

'I'm not scared—'

'None of us is scared of the woods,' Volker said and winked. 'Have you noticed that the houses in every village are built close together?'

The boys glanced around them.

'Farms and fields surround the villages, but the houses are built in a cluster at the centre. It's our way of protecting ourselves from people who pop out unexpectedly from behind the trees.'

'Who would do that?'

'The enemy.'

'What enemy?'

'Each generation has a different one.'

The boys were silent. 'Have you two taught your cousin about the trees?'

'I told him there are places where we have to be careful, but I haven't taken him to the woods near Romehnen yet,' Karl said.

'Long ago all Samlanders were given a tree at birth,' Volker told Otto. 'For men it was usually an oak and for women a linden, the goddess of fate. Once you had your tree, it could never be cut down – if it was, its owner's life would be cut short.'

'Just like that?' Otto asked.

'You'd be surprised at the power of a tree. When I was a few years older than you boys I was taking a short cut back through the forest from Fischhausen when I heard someone scream. It was my brother's voice. I tried to work out where he was and remembered a grove with an old oak in the middle. Our father had told us not to go there and I knew where those screams were coming from. I found my brother pinned under the trunk of a tree that had fallen. His pelvis was crushed and the ground round him was soaked with blood. Even with an axe and three men it would have taken too long to move the tree. He knew that, and so did I.

'I went to the back of the tree where he couldn't see me and tried to pull my knife out without him hearing, but I started to cry. I knew he heard because he fell quiet. We had made a vow to each other years earlier that if either of us was so badly hurt that there was no possibility of recovery, the other would help. I slid up over the fallen trunk, hoping he was looking out into the forest, but he was staring straight into my eyes. I could tell he knew that I was going to keep my vow. I sliced into his neck as fast and deep as I could, then fell on my knees and prayed.'

The boys shuddered and looked at each other without speaking.

Volker bowed his head and went on, 'My father learned the following week that my brother's birth tree, in the village where he had been born near Elbing, had been felled for firewood by a family who had moved there.' Then he pointed at a tree near the edge of the field. 'You see that one?'

The boys nodded.

'That's mine. I keep an eye on it to make sure no one goes near it.'

The boys were aghast.

'Come with me for a moment,' Volker said. The boys hesitated, then did as told. He led them to a grove, pointed to a juniper and a willow, then walked over to the latter and broke off three small switches. He handed one to each boy. 'I don't think you'll need them, but they'll protect you against evil,' he said.

When they started for home, the woods seemed darker than they had earlier, even though the sun was high in the noon sky.

Otto no longer minded that Karl was in front. He and Peter followed close behind, holding their willow switches. Their footsteps rustled leaves and snapped twigs, and for a long time those were the only sounds they could hear – until there was a sudden crack a short distance ahead. A wild boar appeared, glanced at them and ran in the opposite direction.

'Maybe we should go on to the road,' Peter said.

They turned right and pushed through the thick undergrowth until they found themselves on a track that ran through the forest to Germau. When they finally reached the square, they carefully leaned their switches against the iron railing that surrounded the linden and ran for the butcher's.

Chapter 6

After their trip to Ellerhaus the boys avoided the forest and instead hiked to their grandfather's house at Sorgenau, going along the main road through wide pastures and tunnels of neatly planted lindens lining the road. Before, Karl and Peter had paid little attention to them, but now they wondered if spirits lived in those trees as well, even though they weren't in the forest and didn't form a natural grove. They avoided the lone oak in a field a little way from Sorgenau, which Karl and Peter had often climbed.

One day after lunch with their grandfather and his wife, they went to the beach to collect amber. Occasionally someone found a large nugget, but since almost everyone from the villages collected it, they usually found only a few shards, which they took home to Ida. She would take a piece of hardboard, paint a background, then carefully stick the amber to a thin layer of glue to make a sun or breakers crashing on to the beach – made of real sand – with tiny amber people standing on the shore.

On the way back to their grandfather's house Karl had an idea. He would be the Kameradschaftsführer, the sergeant, of their miniature Hitler Youth unit, and told Peter and Otto to stand to attention. Near Sorgenau the cliff was similar to the one he had jumped off, but not so high. When he had persuaded them to play his game, he led them to the cliff. 'You'll probably be the only ones in your group who'll have trained for the test of courage,' he said. 'You'll thank me then.'

He called Otto forward first. His cousin raised his right arm and shouted 'Heil Hitler', as Karl had instructed.

'You see that area over there? I want you to run as fast as you can and jump off without looking down.'

'Can I look first?'

'If you do, what's the point in jumping?'

'But what if I land on the rocks?'

Karl called his brother forward.

'Heil Hitler,' Peter shouted, arm in the air.

'I'll let you keep my knife for the rest of the day if you run across the field and jump without looking.'

'That's not fair!' Otto complained. 'You didn't say that to me.'

'I was going to, but you wouldn't jump. You lost your chance.'

'What if I go after Peter?'

'Here's a better idea. You run together. The first to jump off the cliff keeps it for the rest of today and the other can have it tomorrow.'

Peter and Otto took off.

'Hey! You didn't wait for my order!'

They didn't look back, just continued to race across the field. Peter disappeared over the cliff, then Otto.

Karl stood alone in the field, absorbed in the view across the grass to the sea. His eyes were trained on a ship near the horizon – was it real or a mirage? Then he saw something move near the lip of the cliff. It was Peter, climbing into the field. Then Otto appeared and a moment later they were running towards him. When he realised they were coming for his knife, he turned and raced for the road to their grandfather's house.

'You cheat!' he heard Otto yell. 'We're going to tell Grandpa.'

Chapter 7

By the time autumn 1944 arrived, the atmosphere around the village had changed. Throughout the day countless army trucks loaded with soldiers sped through the place. The boys no longer played on the square since Peter had almost been run over by a truck. The refugees who had occasionally straggled through the village prior to now, now came in a stream – families, older men and women, mothers and young children carrying satchels bound with rope. Almost all were from further east and had left their homes before the war had reached them, even though leaving was seen as disloyalty to the Führer. With no evacuation order forthcoming, many had fled under cover of darkness.

Karl continued to go to school in Pillau, but the two younger boys were at school closer to home. By now they had overcome the fear of the forest that had developed after their experience in Ellerhaus that summer and were hiking once more through the trees. Recently they had found thin strips of aluminium scattered throughout the woods, even in places far off the trail, and had begun to collect it. One day, in the forest near Trulick, four young soldiers confronted them.

'What are you doing?' one asked.

The boys held up the scraps of metal they had picked up.

'Put it back where you found it – and tell everyone else we'll shoot them if we catch them stealing it.'

The other three soldiers laughed. None looked more than sixteen, but the three boys were scared. Each had a large rifle slung over his shoulder.

When one lunged forward, the three boys screamed and the soldiers laughed even more. When they had all calmed down, one of them explained that the aluminium was intended to disrupt enemy radio transmissions: the soldiers had been ordered to scatter it in case the conflict moved into the area.

'But there's no enemy here,' Karl said.

'We're just following orders.'

'How will the aluminium work?' Karl asked.

'How should I know? Maybe the engineers thought the idea up to keep themselves off the battlefield.' The soldier noticed Karl's knife and asked to see it. Karl slid it out of its sheath and handed it to him. After looking for a moment at the handle, he passed it to the one standing beside him. 'Those were the days,' he said.

The third soldier pocketed it. Karl stared at him in disbelief, then realised there was nothing he could do. He started to speak but his voice cracked and he trailed off before bursting into tears.

'You've got a lot to learn if you're going to cry about something like that,' the soldier said, thrusting the knife, handle first, into Karl's chest.

Karl jumped back in fright.

'Take it and get the fuck out of here before I stab you with it. We see you picking up aluminium again, you won't be asking any more questions about the enemy.'

When they got home, Ida asked why they looked so frightened. Peter told her they had bumped into some soldiers.

'I want you to help me move some food from the pantry to the slaughterhouse attic,' she said.

'Why?' Karl asked.

'Don't ask questions.' She told Peter to run over to the Laufers and ask if they had any spare eggs, then said to the other two, 'Come on, we'll make a start.'

Peter left the house and took the road to the Laufers' farm. As he passed the trail that led to the abandoned shed, he thought of the photographs. He had sneaked out to look at them alone ever since Karl brought them back from his trip. He thought again of the girl with her older brother and mother. He had come to admire her – it was as if the blankness of her face masked bravery, defiance of the camera's intrusion. The photo Karl most often looked at was the one of the half-naked woman – perhaps partly because he knew he shouldn't. It was the only picture that either of them had ever seen of a woman's breasts and they knew they wouldn't come across any others in their village.

Knowing that he wouldn't be able to come to the shed during the winter, especially with soldiers about, Peter decided to risk a last visit. He pushed his way through the undergrowth, stopping every few seconds to make sure no one was around.

Inside the shed, he got out the photographs and took them out into the light. He smiled when his eyes rested on the girl, then flipped to the picture with the woman's breasts, and turned finally to the last one of the men huddling together. Then, instead of returning the photographs to their hiding place, he looked around again to make sure no one was watching and took them into the undergrowth. He searched until he found a large, pointed rock, which he used as a shovel to dig a small hole. He had a final glance at the pictures, squeezed his eyes shut to hold the girl in his mind and let them go. They fell into the hole, the flat, thin prints fluttering on top of one another as they entered their final place of rest. He filled it in, patting the dirt firmly into place, then stood up and listened to make sure once more that he was still alone.

The trip to the shed had taken only five minutes, but he knew that now he must run as fast as he could to the Laufers' place or his mother and brother would be wondering where he was. As he raced back to the main road he was gripped by an unexpected sadness he had never felt before when he was looking at the photographs, but instead of slowing and contemplating it and feeling sadder still, he increased his pace until the only thing he was able to concentrate on was maintaining his speed as he sprinted the rest of the way to the road, then on to the farm for the eggs his mother had requested.

Chapter 8

On 20 October Ida learned that the Russians were across the border and advancing into East Prussia, on German territory for the first time since the beginning of the war. It was a day of payback, of retribution, a day of the dead. The Russian soldiers' celebration continued until, on 5 November, the German army counter-attacked and pushed them back.

To maintain the troops' morale, as they held the enemy at bay, Propaganda Minister Joseph Goebbels exploited the name of a village the Russians had sacked when they swept into Germany: Nemmersdorf, he said, contained rooms filled with dead women and children. Female bodies, arms spread wide, had been nailed to barn doors.

The German public were horrified, but since those events had taken place so far to the east, which many listeners had never visited, most felt relatively secure. Ida, however, had given birth to Peter in Nemmersdorf a decade earlier. Any sense of security she had harboured faded with Goebbels's broadcast. But it wasn't only that the Russians were in Nemmersdorf that frightened her: the British Royal Air Force had sent locust swarms of bombers across the dark skies above Germau on their way to Königsberg, where they had dropped so many bombs that the island on which the cathedral stood in a densely populated area had been flattened. Thousands of civilians and seven hundred years of history had been destroyed in two nights. The bombing raids had been the result, in part, of the Allies' belief that if the German army could not be broken, perhaps the people could. But the Samlanders weren't only being targeted by British bombing and Russian soldiers: they were under attack by their own government. Throughout the war the Ministry of Propaganda had kept civilian spirits high with positive broadcasts. That autumn the propaganda intensified as the Eastern Front retreated towards Berlin. Caught between Goebbels's exhortations and her fear that the Russian army was closing in, Ida couldn't understand why Hitler was still refusing to order East Prussian civilians to evacuate. There was talk of secret weapons: Ida never heard an official report, but her neighbours claimed that Hitler planned to use them to defeat the Russians.

After the Russian offensive in late October and the successful German counter-attack in early November there was a lull. The Russians were rumoured to be reinforcing their troops for a new offensive. General Hans Reinhardt, in charge of defending East Prussia, knew that his troops were outnumbered but not that the Russians had five times the number of assault guns and tanks with which he had been supplied. The Germans had defeated the Russians under similar conditions before – but the Allies had landed in Normandy the previous June. Reinhardt's concern, though, was the Russians: there were bigger scores to settle in the east and the Russian army dwarfed that of the Allies.

From the steppes, millions of soldiers were marching west through the winter. Even if those at the front were killed, they would be replaced by more soldiers multiplying across the steppes behind them. If they died, more would take their place.

The largest army in the history of the world was on the move. The Germans had had their chance on Russian territory: now it was the Russians' turn to discover what they could send home to their families from Germany.

Chapter 9

As winter closed in, numerous East Prussian divisions were reorganising in preparation for the next Russian offensive. In January, when the assault finally came, Clausewitz's maxim, 'a defence is stronger than an offence', failed them: the Russian army was inside East Prussia and this time the Germans couldn't muster a defence or counter-attack strong enough to hold or repel them. In Königsberg, General Lasch, in command of the city, which he had returned to its medieval origin as a fortress, had recently received countless prisoners from Poland's Stuffhof concentration camp and was holding them crammed into a factory near the railway station. He ordered the army to take them to the countryside. In the event that the Russian army succeeded in taking the city on the ground, as the British had already done from above, he wanted no evidence that might incriminate him after the war.

The prisoners were cleared out of the factory and marched along the road to Fischhausen, where they were turned north towards Palmnicken, passing within a kilometre of Germau. At one point the line shambling towards the sea stretched all the way from Fischhausen to the junction near Germau. At a distance they were a rag-tag assembly of women mainly sixteen, seventeen, eighteen years old, some in their twenties and thirties, almost none any older, young women marching along the icy road in tattered clothing with the occasional man scattered among them and, even rarer, a family that had not yet been torn apart. Soldiers moved up and down the line shouting. Many were so weak they were unable to keep up and fell into the snow beside the road. When a woman stopped to help her father, a soldier screamed at them to move on. She hesitated, but leaned down anyway to help him. The soldier lifted his rifle, pointed the muzzle into the woman's face and pulled the trigger. The brutal report issued a stern warning to the others. The soldiers' previously disciplined behaviour had disintegrated into chaos, lawlessness and depravity, as hideous as the Nemmersdorf atrocities, which Goebbels continued to lament as the German army murdered its own civilians.

As the prisoners passed the road leading to Germau and encountered the first grove of lindens, a breeze blew in from the coast. It was whispered that the road ended at the amber mines. A prisoner familiar with the town, however, passed the word that they weren't mines at all – just a huge pit dug in the sand that could easily be filled. The implication of his words sent a tremor rippling down the line. Fear turned to panic. Some stopped, marched forward, then stopped again. A few stepped out of the line, followed by others. Soon scores were scrambling over the snow and running out into fields seeking cover among the distant trees. The soldiers screamed at them to stop, then lowered their guns and fired, spreading bullets far and wide to ensure that those who had reached the centre of the field – halfway to safety – would be dead before the trees could save them.

When the guns stopped firing, those still standing were silent but for the shrieks of the dying and the sobs of children. A few minutes later, as if nothing had happened, the soldiers ordered these prisoners to march on.

An old man from Panjes, who had been walking through the forest to visit his sister, had witnessed the massacre from the woods to which the prisoners had been fleeing. He remained among the trees and watched as the line continued west afterwards. Then he retreated deeper into the forest and took a path that led east. When he emerged on to the road, the procession had long disappeared. On his way down the hill into Germau he saw Karl and Otto in the snow. 'Where does the mayor live?' he asked.

The boys took him to a house opposite the butcher's and Karl knocked at the door. When Mr Mazannek answered, Karl introduced the mayor to the old man.

The boys followed the man into the house where the mayor's wife offered them some warm milk. They sat at a table near the door in the living room while the two men talked on the davenport. The old man, still upset, told him what had happened: a group of Jewish prisoners who had tried to escape on the road to Palmnicken had been shot dead by soldiers monitoring the line.

'They just left them there?' the mayor asked. He seemed far less concerned that the prisoners had been shot than that the soldiers hadn't disposed of the bodies.

'They didn't look like they were coming back.'

'What if the Russians come? There'll be no mercy if they find those bodies. It's too late today to do anything about it, but tomorrow I must arrange for a working party to clean up. Is there anyone in Panjes who can help?'

The old man masked his shock after seeing that the mayor cared little for the murdered prisoners. He knew of no other authority to whom he could report the crime. He wanted to leave the mayor's house, so he said he would ask in his village.

'You'd think that the army could handle its own problems,' the mayor concluded.

The old man stood up to leave. The mayor walked with him to the door, then returned to the living room. 'The Russians will level the whole village if they get here and see that. You can't leave bodies at the side of the road!'

Outside, Otto said, 'I've never seen a dead body lying in a field.'

The boys thought back to their grandmother's funeral, when she had been resting peacefully in her coffin. Karl tried to imagine her sprawled on the ground. 'Neither have I.'

'Should we go?'

'It'll be dark soon. Let's get up early and go before anyone else.'

They found Peter in the living room with Leyna.

'Come upstairs,' Karl muttered to him. When they were in the bedroom he and Otto told him what they had heard.

'We're going in the morning,' Otto said.

Later the tavern owner came to the house, told Ida what had happened and asked if Karl could help them to bury the bodies.

'He's too young,' she said. 'I don't want my child doing any such thing.' She was arguing with the man when Karl stepped forward and said he would go. Ida pointed to the stairs. 'Go to bed! You know perfectly well that you don't interrupt adults.'

Sheepishly, Karl climbed the stairs while his mother argued with the man until eventually he left. That night the boys couldn't get to sleep and it was well past midnight before they drifted off. Peter was the first to wake. At dawn, he slipped out of bed and shook the others.

They dressed quickly and crept downstairs, grabbed their coats from the cupboard near the front door and slid their feet into their boots. Then they opened the door quietly and stepped out into the icy air.

At the edge of the square they looked back to make sure no

one was about. Halfway up the hill, Karl glanced back one last time and all three took to their heels. At the junction they veered right and ran for another kilometre. Ahead they could see the lindens, their branches hanging low over the cobbles, covered with snow.

'Can you see anything?'

'It must be further on.'

They went slowly past the lindens to another stretch of open road.

'What's that?' Peter asked, pointing to a shape in the field to the right.

As they moved forward, slowly now, the outlines of bodies became clearer. Most were to the left of the road. The boys stopped short of a large group of bodies. More lay in the field – far more than they had expected. The nearest ones were lying in grotesque positions. One was halfway up the bank with a leg pointing straight up into the air. They all appeared to have frozen solid.

They examined them in a distant, almost clinical manner, the way Karl had studied the first cow he had watched his father kill. He stared at a woman in front of him, a bullet wound through her chest and another through her head. The blood surrounding each body was covered with a thin layer of snow, little more than frozen dew.

Other than the boys' breathing and the shuffle of their boots, there was no sound and no smell but that of the frozen dawn. The blood, exposed to the night air, was more black than red. The longer they inspected the bodies, looking carefully at one, then another, the less frightened they became. Peter and Otto moved among them as if in a trance, disconnected from the carnage, until they came upon the body of a girl lying face up at the side of the road.

Neither boy spoke but Peter thought of the buried photo-graphs. He studied the face, wondering whether she was the same girl. He decided she wasn't, but this brought him little relief. He realised that even if they weren't the same person, they had probably shared a similar fate.

Karl was looking at four bodies on the opposite side of the nearest bank of snow: the sole of a shoe protruded slightly above it. He jumped on to the drift and looked over to the other side. A man lay there, facing the field. The position of his legs showed that he had just started to run when he was shot. The bullets had passed through his back. There was a trail of blood on top of the snow and a pool below him, partly obscured by his body. Unlike the girls dressed in tattered clothes and wooden shoes, the man's trousers and shoes were cleaner and less worn, as if he had prepared carefully for the march. He looked almost as though he had lain down and drifted off to sleep.

Karl jumped off the bank and walked in a wide arc round the body. Now, he focused on the man's stomach and chest where the bullets had left the body. Unlike the back of his jacket, which had three small holes where the bullets had entered, the front of his coat was tattered. He looked familiar, in the way that a stranger on a city street may. Karl bent forward.

He froze.

Mr Wolff. The coffin maker. The man who had taught him so much. The only adult who had ever treated him as an equal. He had aged since Karl had last seen him. But it was him, Karl knew. Unable to speak, he turned to his younger brother and his cousin. They were still staring at the girl, almost as if they were keeping vigil.

Karl took a deep breath. He struggled to find the right thoughts, but he had already grasped that there were none. He didn't know whether to show the others or to run home. Mr Wolff's eyes were open. His absent gaze held Karl witness to the carnage. Again Karl turned to his cousin and little brother – their eyes still fixed on the girl at their feet, her hair spreading past her shoulders against the crystalline snow as her spirit sailed skywards.

Chapter 10

The following day Landwirt appeared. No one mentioned the killings but he was unusually sombre. The children gathered around him, but he asked Ida to take Peter and Otto inside while he talked to Karl. He and the boy set off up the path to the church. When they reached the graveyard, they stood silently near the graves. Then Landwirt asked, 'Did you see it?'

Karl didn't answer. At first he thought his grandfather might punish him if he said he had, but then the grief he had kept to himself since he had found Mr Wolff's body surfaced and tears ran down his face.

His grandfather stepped closer but didn't touch him. In the distance, where the hill fell away into the forest below, Karl noticed limbs heavy with snow. For a brief moment he felt as if he were encased in a frozen world, in a time and place from which he knew he'd never completely escape. He stood beside his grandfather as they absorbed the frozen silence and the entire world seemed to have come to a stop.

'War is honourable,' Landwirt said. 'We seek new places to live, even if those places are already someone else's home. That is a rule of life and always has been.'

In a moment of clarity, gazing at Landwirt's wooden leg, Karl realised that war had moulded his grandfather's ideas about the world and that now it was doing the same to him – just as it had to his ancestors in a seemingly endless struggle that, to him, was focused on the disputed territories of Central Europe.

Landwirt watched his grandson for a moment longer, then turned to the forest. He sighed. 'There are rules of war, too. Even when the Teutonic Knights conquered this peninsula, they made an effort to uphold them. War takes place between two powers, both armed, both prepared to fight.'

There was another silence, as if Landwirt wasn't sure what to say next. But when he spoke again Karl realised that he knew exactly what he was going to say, as though he had practised as he had walked, on his wooden leg, to Germau that afternoon.

'I'm not going to lie to you. I've never liked Jews. I never thought much of Mr Wolff. I never understood why a Jew would make coffins in a Protestant village. He should have left Christians to bury their own.'

Landwirt looked across to the steeple with the abandoned stork's nest, then at the ground. 'But I never told your mother not to let you visit him. In life you must make up your own mind,' he said, his voice rising. 'You hear about the camps, but they always seem far away. When the SS arrive in your own town and kill Jews in the open, you think differently. Dislike for someone doesn't give me the right to kill him. I've killed men in battle and not once felt guilt over that. But you should not kill people who have done no wrong!'

Karl remained silent. He had never seen his grandfather so upset. When Landwirt reached out, Karl flinched – as if his grandfather had been about to hit him. Then he understood and reached for his grandfather's hand. They went across the field to where the path the children often followed dropped away into the forest. There, Landwirt stopped and looked over the shallow valley. 'I know you have to leave soon. Ida told me you've been given orders.'

Karl looked at his grandfather in a mild state of shock. Like his mother, he had pushed the thought out of his mind. Although Karl's leader had come to the house less than a week ago and told him and his mother, she had not said a word to him about it since – as if by refusing to acknowledge it, the order might go away. But he now realised that she had talked with her father about it afterwards. Karl wondered if Landwirt was about to say that he had succeeded in convincing the youth organisation to let Karl stay with his mother. Especially after the events of the last couple of days. Instead, he said, 'We don't usually expect orders so early in life, but there's little I can do about it. We can only pray that you'll be safe, wherever they take you.'

Karl thought about his grandfather in the battle of Tannenberg – had he been scared when his order came? He tried to pluck up the courage to ask, but his grandfather laid his index finger on his lips to silence him.

Eventually Landwirt let go of his hand and reached into his coat pocket. He held out something to his grandson. 'I want you to have it for your journey.'

Karl opened his hand beneath Landwirt's clenched fist and felt something fall into it. He looked down – the Iron Cross Landwirt had been awarded after the battle of Tannenberg. A piece of string was knotted through the hole that had once held a ribbon.

'You'll soon be on your first journey into war,' Landwirt said. 'We never know what will happen.'

Karl stared at it. The string was just long enough for him to wear the cross round his neck under his uniform. He didn't know what to say. He had asked to see it almost every time he had visited his grandfather, who had told him more than once about its origin: designed by an architect named Schinkel in 1813 during the Wars of Liberation when Prussia was allied with Russia to fight the French who had begun their retreat from Königsberg, having failed already to take Moscow. The medal had been kept hidden on his grandfather's bookshelf in a hollowed-out copy of the Brothers Grimm's tales with the wedding band from his first marriage.

Landwirt helped Karl to slide the string over his head and tuck the cross beneath his shirt. They stood for a while without speaking. 'We had better get back to the house. Your mother's waiting.'

As they walked back across the snowy field, Karl felt the Iron Cross warm against his skin and understood that his life was changing now in a way that was beyond his comprehension and the guidance of his family. The order had been issued. He was going to war.

Chapter 11

The atmosphere in the village changed again that winter, as if the lines strung across each rooftop to stop the storks nesting had been pulled so taut that the slightest additional tension would cause them to snap and the houses beneath to crumble. Ida no longer remembered when she had last heard from her husband and now she needed to talk to him more than ever. She couldn't deal with the news alone. She had just made up her mind to talk with her father about it instead – he would know better what to say to Karl than she – when Karl had startled her that morning to ask if breakfast was ready. 'How many times do I have to tell you that I'll call you when it's on the table?' she snapped. She immediately knew she had overreacted and was ashamed. She had gone to Karl and hugged him. 'I'm sorry.'

It was the same morning that the youth group leader had come to the house and told her that he had orders to inform her and Karl that selected members were to prepare to leave home for leadership training; the others would form a home guard to help the regular army protect the peninsula against the Russians.

'But what about the rest of us?' Ida had asked.

'No transport orders have been issued for civilians.'

'Where do they plan to take the boys?'

'Wherever they're needed.'

'Will he be allowed to see us?'

'That depends. It's an honour for him to go. Not everyone of his age is given the chance.' Then he turned to Karl. 'Report to Pillau on Friday morning at nine. Don't be late.'

During his last two days at home, after Landwirt had talked with Karl, she let him listen to whatever music he chose. He played his favourite record over and over again. The family stayed up late: Peter hammered out a tune in his brother's honour on the piano, Leyna fell asleep on the couch, and all the boys ate so much cake that they had to lie on the floor, holding their stomachs.

The next morning, Ida told everyone to put on their coats and boots: they would go for a family walk. As they walked north from the square, Salomo ran outside but Karl told him he wanted to be alone with his family.

Ida had promised herself that she wouldn't worry about anything all day – she didn't want to make Karl anxious. In the crisp morning air as they walked across rolling land covered with a thick blanket of snow, she felt strangely serene and took hold of Karl's hand. After a few moments Karl pulled away from her. He was too old for that, especially in front of Peter and Otto. When they reached a rise where they could see across the fields they stopped. 'This must be the most beautiful place on earth,' Ida said.

'What about Africa?' Otto asked.

'Well, I've never been there, but I imagine it's beautiful, too. What do you think?' she asked the others.

'I like it here,' Karl said. 'It's home. But Father likes it here, too, and he had to go away for a while.'

'We'll have a big party when you come home,' Ida said. 'Maybe you and your father will come back together.'

'I wonder if I'll ever go anywhere?' Peter asked.

'You can come to see me in Berlin,' Otto told him.

'When things calm down, we'll all go to see Elsa in Berlin,' Ida promised.

Back at the house the boys lounged around in the living room, listening to music again. During the afternoon Ida ironed Karl's uniform and packed a small suitcase with an extra pair of shoes and more clothing. She also made a picnic for him to take on the train and stored it in a box on the back porch to keep cool. When the boys fell asleep that night on the living-room floor, Ida decided not to wake them. She had already brought blankets downstairs for Leyna, who was asleep in a corner, and went back upstairs for more, carried them down and spread them over the boys. Then she lay down on the davenport and pulled a blanket over herself.

Karl woke first when it was still dark. He roused Ida. 'I should start getting ready. I don't want to miss the train.'

'Give me a minute, sweetheart.'

Ida rubbed her eyes. She remembered sitting on the steps of her in-laws' home with Karl when he was a baby, wondering how she would feel when he grew up and left home. She had imagined him married, then as a young father, herself a grand-mother, as her son prepared to move with his wife and child down to the Masurian lakes to begin his butcher's apprentice-ship, as all the men on both sides of the family had for gener-ations. She had seen herself holding her grandchild while her son and his wife finished packing.

She had never imagined that he would be only twelve when he went. But she knew there was nothing she could do now. They would come to get him if he wasn't at the station. Besides, he wanted to go. And even if he didn't, he would never disobey a direct order. He might disobey her, but the group had a stronger influence on him – which she did not altogether like. She had never seen him as proud as he had been on the day he had come back from camp after his initiation into the youth group. He had seemed more man than boy somehow, his childish innocence fading.

When Peter and Otto woke, Ida stood up and turned on the light, then picked up Leyna and sat her on the couch. 'Peter, help her put her clothes on while I get ready.'

Karl had already placed his suitcase next to the front door. He was sitting at the table, in his uniform, eating a piece of cold sausage when Ida came in. She went to the back porch to retrieve the food she had made for his journey.

When she returned to the living room Peter and Otto were ready. Peter was buttoning Leyna's coat while Otto tied his bootlaces. Everything seemed to be happening at once. Ida had hoped they would have a few final moments of peace together before they left for the station, but everyone, including Karl, was standing in the middle of the room, waiting for her.

Ida looked at her older son in the long coat one of the older boys had given him, his hands buried in his pockets. 'I've forgotten something,' she said and rushed out of the room. She went upstairs into her bedroom, shut the door and stood in front of the bureau. Her eyes filled with tears. What had she done to deserve this? Was God punishing her for some sin she had committed unwittingly? But she couldn't keep Karl waiting nervously downstairs. She pulled herself together and wiped away the tears. When she went down, she was holding her coat in front of her as if she had gone upstairs to fetch it.

Karl could see that his mother had been crying. There was

an awkward moment of silence. Then she asked, 'Have we got everything?'

Sadness rose in Karl when he heard the sorrow in her voice. But, like his mother, he knew he had to be strong. He was the oldest boy there and he did not want anyone to see him cry in his uniform. He turned to the door and opened it.

Cold air swept into the room. The morning light barely illuminated the square but he could see the trees, the path up to the church, the mayor's house, the road to the station, each image etching itself into his mind. He wanted to hold that picture until the day he died.

Instead of taking the path, they followed the road. Peter had insisted on carrying Karl's suitcase and they walked in silence. When they reached Kirpehnen, they turned right towards Powayen and soon saw the railway station. Other families were already gathering on the platform. Half a dozen boys, in neat uniforms, were huddled with their mothers, younger brothers and sisters. Some stood silently, holding each other's hands, while others talked excitedly.

Peter asked if Karl would write to them.

'Of course, but you have to write to me too.'

'Where do I send my letter?'

'I'll let you know when I get there.'

Ida tried to think of something to say before the train arrived, but it was already coming down the track. A woman nearest to them, alone with her only son, began to cry. Ida took several deep breaths to keep her own tears at bay. She grabbed Karl's hand.

As soon as the train stopped, the guard shouted to the boys that they should board now. The younger children gathered around Karl. Ida reached out and brushed a particle of ice off his cheek. He shook hands with Peter and Otto, bent down to kiss Leyna, then turned to his mother. The guard was shouting again. Ida took him in her arms and held him to her. As he stepped away from her to board the train, she looked into his eyes and, without letting her voice betray her words to be anything but the truth, said, 'We're so proud of you.'

BOOK III

The Circular Path

Chapter 1

In early February 1945 Landwirt arrived at his daughter's house, having hobbled along the icy road from Sorgenau. Russian troops were now well inside East Prussia and due to break through to the peninsula. Two weeks earlier they had launched a giant pincer offensive to sever East Prussia from the rest of Germany. The northern claw was now closing on the peninsula while the southern one pierced the mainland opposite the bay. The German Army Group Centre, defending East Prussia, was now behind enemy lines, perfectly positioned for destruction by the swelling Soviet divisions approaching from all directions – the First Baltic Army Group from the north, the Third Belarusian Army Group from the west and the Second Belarusian Army Group from the south-east, a force of well over a million men.

In the final week of January Landwirt had heard from a retreating soldier that the Russians had taken Tannenberg. He knew that if the army couldn't hold a place as symbolic as Tannenberg, they couldn't hold anywhere else.

What Landwirt didn't know was that with the German Army Group Centre now cut off from the west, the General Staff had decided to rename it Army Group North. It consisted of forty-one divisions split into three secondary armies: the Second Field

Army, the Fourth Field Army and the Third Panzer Army, the last ordered to defend the Samland peninsula. On the morning that Landwirt rushed to Germau to make sure his daughter was ready, the General Staff, a thousand kilometres away, was approving a new decision to rename the Third Panzer Army Operational Group Samland. Since there was no possibility of retreat, backed up as they were against the sea on three sides, the group's objective needed no clarification from the high command: defend Samland at all costs.

Also unknown to Landwirt, on the previous day the American secretary of state and the British foreign minister had met in Malta to discuss, among other things, the disintegration of East Prussia as a territorial unit. When Roosevelt, Churchill and Stalin gathered three days later in Yalta, they tacitly confirmed that this would take place. Landwirt had walked to Germau every day during the previous week to keep abreast of the breaking news: soldiers were now the only reliable source, the radio's façade of truth long since destroyed. His grandchildren had reported hearing rumbling at night from artillery to the east, but the boys were no longer allowed to hike in the woods to investigate.

The women went about their daily business as if each day were like any other, but beneath the mask of calm lay anxiety that prompted them to hoard food caches throughout the village. Refugees continued to pass through the square, but the villagers no longer offered them anything to eat. The Führer still hadn't issued the evacuation order they had expected a month ago. The mayor, the only fervent Party member left in the village, warned against escape – it was officially condemned as defeatist. Most villagers still hoped that their troops would be victorious, but they kept hearing of ships loaded with refugees departing from Pillau to be sunk by Soviet submarines.

Three days earlier the *Wilhelm Gustloff* had left Gotenhafen loaded with East Prussian refugees, many of whom had crossed the bay from Pillau in smaller boats. It was torpedoed and almost everyone on board was drowned. The villagers had known people on the ship but no one would utter their names. The more deaths they heard about, the more they had to protect themselves. Shortly afterwards, Ida had overheard two boys from a neighbouring village talking about a tragedy that had occurred even closer to home on the night after the *Gustloff* had sunk. She had stopped to listen, but they had fallen silent.

When Landwirt appeared later that afternoon she asked, 'Has something happened near the coast? I overheard some boys talking this morning about the amber mines.'

Landwirt went towards the kitchen. 'Have you seen my watch?' he asked. 'I think I left it last time I was here.'

'I asked you a question, Vati!'

He said nothing.

She thought of Karl. 'What are you hiding from me?'

Landwirt stared at the floor.

'If those boys this morning know about it you must tell me,' she said, getting angry.

'That's the problem,' he said. 'They had boys over there.'

'*What* boys?'

Landwirt knew his daughter wouldn't stop questioning him until he had told her everything he knew. But before he had a chance, Ida said angrily, 'Why does everyone pretend they don't know anything!'

'Sometimes it's just too much to take in,' Landwirt said.

'Silence is worse.'

While rescue boats were still recovering floating bodies from the *Gustloff* disaster, whose numbers were mounting to the highest death toll in maritime history, a large group of young

Jewish women in Palmnicken were told that a ship large enough to carry all of them had arrived. It was waiting – their second apparent piece of luck. The first had occurred when they had survived the death march from Königsberg. A landowner named Hans Ansbach had kept the survivors in a manufacturing building close to the amber mines to keep them safe from the local mayor, who was loyal to the SS. As commander of the Palmnicken Volkssturm, Ansbach had made clear that they were not to be executed.

The mayor, however, hatched a different plan. With the help of an SS officer he sent a telegram to Ansbach, telling him to take his militia unit and race east to help a group of German soldiers under attack by the Russians. Ansbach had departed immediately but he didn't get very far – his body was later found in the forest. The mayor had then taken charge of the prisoners.

There was an audible excitement in the room when they were told to get ready to go to the beach where the ship was waiting. But as they went towards the sea, a group was split off from the main bunch without being told why and directed towards the amber mines.

Panic ensued.

Those forced to continue to the beach saw no ship. Before most had time to flee, SS guards fanned out behind them under cover of the cliffs and opened fire with their machine-guns, driving the women out into the icy Baltic waters. Those not killed by bullets died of hypothermia. The group sent to the mine had been led, one at a time, to the pit and told to kneel beside it. As if in an abattoir a man clinically pressed a gun at the back of their heads. One after the other, they slumped forward into the pit. Afterwards, the mayor sent a few Hitler Youth into the surrounding forests to search for the girls who escaped while being led to the beach. The boys were armed but received no orders to bring them back.

Ida began to feel sick. She thought again of Karl. It's not possible, she hoped. But she had no idea where he had been since he had left. Suddenly her throat constricted. She pushed past Landwirt and ran out of the house into the woods and vomited. Now she understood why her father hadn't wanted to answer.

She realised that she had to concentrate now on saving the children – Peter, Leyna and Otto. Her father had already told her that he didn't have the strength to escape. She would be on her own.

She avoided thinking about leaving her father behind. Once she had recovered, Ida had said, 'Maybe things will turn round and we won't have to go.'

'Anything's possible,' he answered, without much enthusiasm.

Landwirt had then promised her that he would stay hidden now in Sorgenau until the danger passed.

She was startled the next day to see her father crossing the square when she glanced out of the window. 'I thought I told you not to come back!' she said as he let himself into the living room.

'Any news?'

'Same as yesterday. They're a few kilometres east. You know they'll kill any men they find.'

'I don't think they'll waste ammunition on an old man with one leg. I've fought the Russians before.'

'I'd rather you didn't take the risk. I don't want the children to see you killed.'

'Where are the boys?'

'Upstairs. I'll call them down, but then you must go.' She walked to the foot of the stairs and called Peter and Otto. Then she turned back to Landwirt. 'Please don't be long. You know you shouldn't be here.'

'Come here, my angel.' He held out his arms and she went into his embrace. He hugged her to his chest. 'When they arrive, I want you to do exactly as I told you.'

She nodded, pressing her face into her father's shoulder, eyes shut. She allowed herself to relax against him, then pulled away. She half smiled and said, 'We'll be all right, I promise. It's you I'm worried about.'

'I'll go now. I just wanted to see you one last time. Now I'll spend a minute with the boys. You'll need their help.'

She nodded and went into the kitchen. Landwirt heard pans being moved on the stove. The boys ran downstairs, excited that their grandfather had returned. Leyna had come into the room a little before them and smiled at him shyly. She was more like Paul than her mother, he thought. 'Come and sit on my lap, little one,' he said.

With the two boys on either side of him he said, 'You know the woods well. Don't let any loud noise frighten you if you get lost. The artillery never know exactly where they're firing.'

'Are you coming with us, Grandpa?' Leyna asked.

He laid a hand on his granddaughter's head and continued talking to the boys: 'Your mother needs you to be strong, so no crying.'

Ida returned with a small bag of food for her father's walk back to Sorgenau. 'Give Jiera our love,' she said.

Landwirt stood up and hugged them all. 'I'll be back tomorrow,' he said. Then he kissed his daughter one last time and left. A few minutes later it was as if he had never been there and the boys were asking when lunch would be ready.

'Later.'

An hour after Landwirt had left, Peter and Otto again heard

artillery firing, towards Willkau, the explosions and gunshots becoming louder, moving towards their village, dying away, then beginning anew. They sat on the floor in the living room, peering out of the window at the deserted square, listening to the fighting for two more hours, as Ida prepared a meal. Before she called the children to the table, she took the warm rolls from the oven and put them on a plate. She returned to the kitchen for the Speck just as the boys yelled, 'They're here!'

She nearly dropped it, then heard her father's voice: *Ida, my dear child, don't panic when they arrive. Whatever you do, don't panic.* She went into the living room and sat on the davenport, calling Leyna to sit on her lap. She was in a mild state of shock.

The boys watched Russian soldiers goose-step on to the square. Peter was afraid but intrigued too. He had expected the Russians to run into the village, one at a time, hiding behind trees, shooting out windows, as an enormous T-38 tank chugged behind them, stopping and swinging its turret while the cannon searched out targets.

Instead, an orderly line of soldiers laid claim to the village, as though they were practising a field manoeuvre. When they reached the centre the front guard fanned out to search for pockets of resistance, while a horse-drawn artillery piece was stationed in the square. It began to fire over the houses into fields to the north, where German units were apparently still concentrated. The T-38 never arrived.

Chapter 2

As the boys watched the soldiers firing, the mayor stepped calmly out of his house. Holding a white handkerchief in the air and wearing his Nazi uniform, he marched towards the Russian commander as if to settle peace terms. He received them, but not the ones he had perhaps anticipated: three soldiers grabbed his arms and a fourth tossed a rope over one of the lower branches of the linden tree. The mayor was promptly strung up and left hanging. As Landwirt had predicted, no bullets were wasted.

When the body had gone limp, the boys ducked below the windowsill, but soon were peering out again as more troops converged on the square. Ida sat on the davenport, plaiting Leyna's hair. At first she had left the boys to watch what was going on outside, but now she told them to come and sit with her.

'But what if they come in?' Peter asked.

'Come now!'

She stared at the clock on the wall. It appeared to have stopped at 10.44. After an eternity, the minute hand crept forward: 10.45. She concentrated on Leyna's hair and waited. The sound finally came: the creak and clank of the front gate opening, then slamming shut. Shuffling feet. Heavy footsteps up to the door.

It burst open. Following her father's advice, Ida had left it unlocked. *Don't resist. Things will only be worse.* Four soldiers came in, barely glancing at Ida and the three children. With their guns drawn, one went into the kitchen, another into the shop and two others ran upstairs. Ida listened to doors being opened and shut, heavy footsteps moving from room to room, the thump of objects hitting the floor, as they searched for men. Leyna sat on her mother's lap, holding the teddy bear her grandfather had given her. Ida ran her fingers through the little girl's hair.

She concentrated on nearby objects to control her fear as her father had told her. She stared at her fingernails – she hadn't trimmed them since Christmas Eve. She didn't want to betray her fear to the children, who kept glancing at her as if they were waiting to be told what to do. Then she returned to Leyna's long hair.

One by one the soldiers came back to the living room. They gestured the family away from the sofa. Two soldiers looked behind, then beneath the furniture. When they were certain that no men were hiding in the house they motioned for Ida and the children to sit down again. The leader asked in Russian whether there were any men in the village.

Ida recalled the Masurian dialect her parents had sometimes spoken and its Slavic approximations. In broken sentences, she tried to explain that the men had been gone for years. Then he asked if she had any liquor. Landwirt had taken it away more than a week before. What he couldn't carry to Sorgenau he had poured away near the slaughterhouse. She pretended not to understand the question.

After a period of silence, one of the soldiers asked her to show him something upstairs. Again she pretended she didn't understand. He asked again, then approached her. She stopped him by setting Leyna to the side and asking the boys to watch her while she went upstairs. She calmly started up the stairs, followed by two soldiers. The children huddled on the sofa, while the other two men continued to look behind furniture, opening and closing drawers. One put a record he had found beneath the davenport on the turntable and tried to switch it on, but there was no electricity: an explosion that morning had severed the power lines to the village.

Fifteen minutes later Ida and the men came downstairs as another man walked in through the front door. The four soldiers stood to attention. The newcomer glanced at the two on the stairs behind Ida and shouted something. They cowered and left the house. The officer waved his handgun as though he had forgotten he was holding it. Unlike the other men, he spoke fluent German: he complimented Ida on her home, sat in a chair opposite the family and focused on Leyna, fiddling in his pocket. Finally he produced a small piece of chocolate. Ida saw that it had been made by a company in Königsberg – it was sold throughout the peninsula. He asked Ida if he could give Leyna some. She stood the little girl on the floor in front of her. At first Leyna held on to her mother's knee, but soon she crossed the narrow distance to the man. As soon as she reached him, he leaned down, picked her up, sat her on his lap and gave her the chocolate. Then he began to talk. 'I have a little girl of her age at home. I haven't seen her for four years.'

Ida didn't ask if he missed them. Instead, she asked how many children he had, what colour their hair was, where they lived. 'You'll be able to go home soon,' she said. 'The war must be almost over.'

He glanced at the piano in the corner of the room. 'Who plays?'

'My son.'

The Flight

The officer waved his hand that still gripped the gun at Peter. 'We should have a song,' he said. He named three or four, but Peter didn't know them. Finally he said, 'What about "Ich hatt' einen Kameraden".'

Peter, of course, knew that one. His father and grandfather knew it too, as did every member of the Hitler Youth. At that moment, though, it didn't matter that everyone knew it because Peter was too nervous to play, let alone sing. It wasn't until he concentrated on the sheet music resting on the shelf in front of him that his hands steadied.

When he reached the end the officer said, 'Again,' waving his gun in the air for emphasis. Peter started to play and this time the officer began to sing in perfect tune to Peter's accompaniment. As he listened to the Russian officer singing, he discovered meaning in the song. He had never paid much attention to the lyrics until he heard the emotion in the man's voice:

> In battle he was my comrade,
> None better have I had.
> When the drum called us to fight,
> He was always on my right,
> In step, through good and bad.
> A bullet flew towards us,
> For him or meant for me?
> His life from mine it tore,
> At my feet a piece of gore,
> As if a part of me.
> He reached up to hold my hand.
> I must reload my gun.
> I cannot ease your pain, my friend,
> For in afterlife we'll meet again,
> And walk once more as one.

When he reached the end, he hoped the man wouldn't ask him to repeat it a third time, but the officer said in a fatherly voice, 'Thank you, my son.'

For a little while they sat in silence, Peter on the piano stool, the officer with Leyna on his lap, Ida and Otto on the sofa. The cannon in the square fired intermittently. Voices shouted. The officer was clearly exhausted – he appeared not to have slept for days. From the piano stool, Peter watched the commotion outside. Villagers were being directed to the church. Another officer was running around, shouting to the soldiers, until another stopped him and pointed to the butcher's. He turned, saw Peter through the window, charged through the front gate and into the house. He shouted something in Russian to the first officer, turned and went out.

'I have to be going,' the officer said. 'Put on some warm clothes. They want you to go up the hill to the church with your neighbours.'

He stood Leyna on the floor and she ran across the room to Ida. Before he left he turned to Ida and said, 'God bless you.'

As soon as he was out of the house, Ida told the children to get ready. They had already practised dressing for a fast departure. Ida had made sure, following Landwirt's instructions, that everyone had warm clothing ready. Leyna's were stacked beside the sofa and she began to pull them on to her daughter hastily while the boys ran upstairs.

Chapter 3

Within minutes everyone was dressed and in the living room. Ida had slipped on two sweaters and buttoned her long wool coat. The family stepped through the front door into the cold yard, walked down the steps and passed through the gate. As it clanked shut behind them, a group of soldiers turned. Two female soldiers pointed at Ida's boots. She returned to the porch, sat down and untied them. As she handed the first to the soldier standing nearest, she saw the other woman looking at her coat. She unlaced the second boot, handed it over, then slipped off her coat. The women left her sitting in her stockings as they turned to go back through the gate. Ida ran inside, retrieved a pair of worn workboots from the back porch, found an old, worn coat and rejoined the children.

Her hands started trembling. She tried to push the thought of the soldiers in her bedroom out of her mind, but the image of them standing over her sharpened. She was succumbing now to the shock, which spread through her. She made herself focus on the square, which was filled with soldiers – more people than had been present even for the celebration on the day Paris had fallen. Soldiers were still pouring in from the road to the east. Landwirt had told her repeatedly to leave the centre of the village as early as she could to avoid the evening celebration, which was sure to follow the fall of Germau.

A number of soldiers were unlike any she had ever seen before, their features more Asiatic than European. She remembered the stories her father had told her about the Mongolian warriors under Genghis Khan, whose rule had once reached eastern Europe, and the Huns under Attila, who had reached the west. Paul had said that the German army had units of French, Danish and Latvian soldiers, and she realised that the Russian army included people from other countries too. That day the village seemed not only the centre of the war, but of the world with so many cultures converging to plot their separate journeys to survival. The boys tugged Ida along towards the path up the hill where everyone was gathering.

When they reached the other villagers, Ida saw the woman who owned the blacksmith's, with her two children beside a larger group. 'Liselotte!' Ida called. The woman turned. 'We need to get away from here.'

'They told us to come here,' Liselotte said, clutching her two children to her. 'We should do as they say.'

'We have done. Are you prepared to wait while they decide what to do with us next?'

'We have no choice.'

'Come with us.'

'I don't think—'

'We haven't much time,' Ida said.

'I'll stay here for now—'

'And let them lock you into the church? Then they'll be able to do whatever they want.'

Liselotte turned back to the group waiting to go into the church. Ida glanced down at the square: five soldiers were marching more villagers up the hill. She told the children to follow her and moved slowly and cautiously to the back of the church through the cemetery and into the woods. There, Peter and Otto took the lead. Once more Landwirt's voice was in Ida's mind: *Don't follow anyone to the west. You'll never outrun the troops. Go behind the enemy line into their territory. There's always a vacuum of power there. At least at first, it's where you'll be safest.* The family was heading east, into the interior. If there was a power vacuum behind the line, Ida knew, there would also be lawlessness. She pushed away the thought and concentrated on the plans they had made earlier in the week. Soon the trees thinned and they were standing at the edge of a frozen pond. On the other side an old man held a hunting rifle. Volkssturm – the so-called people's army – she decided, but he had no interest now in defending East Prussia for Hitler.

'Where are they?' he asked.

'In Germau.'

They started across the ice towards him, but he waved them back. 'Your tracks. They'll find me if they're following you.' He pointed north. 'The road should be clear. If somebody comes through here after you, I'll stop them.'

Ida called out in the old language a Balt-Prussian proverb, which she was sure he would understand: 'God gives teeth, God gives bread.' The man bowed his head, but said nothing. A few seconds later he peered into the woods behind them, then waved his rifle: they should go on while he remained behind to guard the forest. The family crossed the ice without looking back.

In the woods again, they brushed under the trees, heavy with snow. At first Ida kept pace with the boys, but when a fallen branch touched her leg she jerked back and stopped. The children turned and she started to speak, but faltered. She knew that if she was to overcome what had happened to her in the bedroom she had to do so now. The children depended on her.

She closed her eyes briefly, then told the boys to keep moving and reached down for Leyna's hand.

A few minutes later Peter stopped at the edge of a clearing. They looked carefully up and down the empty field, walked into the open and crossed to the road. Ida realised they had already bypassed Krattlau and Willkau. Her father had told her to try to reach Thierenberg that evening. At that moment she saw three bodies lying beside the road – Germans, from their uniforms. She hesitated, then overtook Peter, who was staring at them, transfixed. They passed three more bodies and came upon more, of much younger men this time. Ida thought of Karl. The second group of five or six had apparently been hit by the same spray of machine-gun fire, because they had fallen so close to one another.

'See if they have identification. Their mothers will want to know,' Ida said.

Peter and Otto moved among the bodies. Peter slid his hand into a soldier's pocket. It was empty. He jumped away. He ran back to his mother. Otto looked up the road to where more bodies were scattered about. Ida gathered the children and led them away, hoping they would soon be beyond the carnage. As the family moved east along the cobbled road through scattered bodies, civilians began climbing out from hiding places in the bushes edging the roadside to go along with them.

Chapter 4

Within an hour of finding the dead soldiers they had been joined by eight people from nearby villages who were also moving east. Two young women, three older ones and three girls. Ida was worried now that the group was too large and would easily be seen from a distance, so she led them off the road towards a farmhouse owned by a friend of her father's. Halfway across a field she realised that a scout might spot their tracks.

Peter pointed ahead. 'Let's go through the trees.'

'You boys go first and I'll bring up the rear to make sure everyone stays together.'

When they reached the house it was filled with women, children and two men. Before she introduced herself, Ida told them to put out the fire they had built. 'They'll see the smoke.'

But many people in the room were shivering: they had been hiding in the forest. The boy who was tending the flames ignored her.

Ida pushed Leyna and the boys over to the fire to warm up, then took the three to the edge of the room and sat down, before telling Otto and Peter to go and look out of the window.

'Mother!' Peter shouted.

A small group of Russian soldiers was coming over the hill.

A commissar sat in a horse-drawn sleigh that he must have taken from an abandoned farm, led by six soldiers on horseback, riding two abreast.

They were trapped, Ida knew. They had run from one group of enemy soldiers into the arms of another. When the soldiers reached the house, they stopped and fanned out. The officer signalled to his men to encircle the house, while he remained in his sleigh at the front. Then he shouted an order in German: the women were to step on to the front porch. 'Don't make us come to fetch you.'

Ida told the children to gather in circles round their mothers. This time everyone did as she suggested, since only she had developed a plan. Then each group went out on to the porch. The children gathered round the women. The two men remained inside.

'Are there any men?' the officer shouted.

The two old men shuffled out.

'Any more?'

One man shook his head.

'You can stay here for the night,' the officer said, 'but in the morning you must go to the crossroads east of here and a truck will take you to the station for evacuation.'

He pulled at the sleigh reins and called for three of the soldiers to come with him up the road. The others, who had returned to the front of the house, remained on their horses. At first Ida wasn't sure what their presence meant. *They're to guard us*, she decided.

The soldiers took their horses to a tree near the front porch, where they tied them up. As they did so, they told everyone, in Russian, to go back inside. At first no one moved. Then a child stepped inside and slammed the door behind her. Everyone jumped. The girl's mother followed her in, then the two old men.

Guns drawn, the soldiers pushed the rest of the group inside and entered the house. They motioned everyone into the front room, then searched it. When they returned, the women were sitting on two sofas.

The soldiers glanced around the room and muttered a few words to each other. The tallest of the three approached a woman and reached for her hand. As she stood up, her daughter asked, 'Where is he taking you?' Then to the soldier, 'Mutti doesn't want to go with you.'

But the woman was already standing. The soldier pulled at her right hand, while her daughter and the boy beside her grabbed the other. The peculiar tug-of-war took place until eventually the soldier released her hand. She and the two children fell backwards on to the sofa.

The next woman on the couch was Ida. The soldier grasped her arm and yanked her to her feet. When Otto and Peter tried to hold her back, the soldier pointed his gun at them and took her out of the room.

The rest listened to footsteps climb the stairs. A door opened, then clicked shut. Silence descended. Soon they heard a faint, persistent rustling noise, like a mouse gnawing on the wooden floor above.

The two soldiers left to stand guard gazed out of the window. When their comrade reappeared he was alone. Another soldier went out and climbed the stairs. The faint rhythmic sound started again. A little girl asked her mother when they would eat. A boy wanted to know if he could go outside. A third child began to cry. When the second soldier returned the three talked together, then addressed the room in Russian and departed.

Peter and Otto ran to the stairs and found Ida already at the bottom of the flight.

'Did they hurt you?' Peter asked.

'Where's Leyna?'

They returned to the front room. Nobody mentioned the soldiers. No one asked Ida any questions or tried to comfort her. Instead, everyone pretended that nothing had happened. A man added more turf to the dying fire.

After a moment Ida announced that she needed to go outside. Peter followed her on to the porch. 'If you're coming with me, tell Otto to look after Leyna.'

Peter ran inside, then rejoined his mother.

Just then, Ida became aware of cows bellowing in the barn. 'Their udders are full,' she said.

Ida went into the barn, approached the nearest cow and began to spray milk into the hay. Then she stopped and searched for a bucket. She told Peter to start milking too. When the bucket was full, she set it in the middle of the floor, found another bucket and moved on to the next cow. She had fallen into a trance, when she felt someone touch her shoulder. She whirled round. One of the men from the living room stood behind her. 'Come now,' he said. 'That's enough. You should be inside.'

Reluctantly, Ida followed him. Then, unable to ignore the bellowing of the cows that still hadn't been milked, she told Peter to go back and finish the job. He started to cry.

The old man was irritated. 'What's the matter with you?'

Ida went back to Peter, calmed him and said to the man, 'We need to finish milking. Will you help?'

'Let's get on with it then,' he said.

At last they returned to the house, carrying three buckets of milk. The old man took them into the kitchen where he opened and closed cupboards until he had found the glasses, which he took down and lined up on the table. He was filling the glasses when Otto entered the kitchen with Leyna, looking for Ida and Peter.

The other man appeared and told Ida to come into the living room. 'Just for a minute,' he said. 'We'll have the milk afterwards.'

When everyone was present the man said, 'What should we do if the soldiers come back?'

A woman at the back of the room said, 'There's a gap under the floor of a cupboard. The four girls could squeeze into it together.'

'What about the little ones?' one of the mothers asked.

'They should be safe here.'

'But what about us?' another asked.

Nobody answered. The men blushed. 'She's right,' Ida said. 'We must make sure the older girls are safe. Ursula', she said, taking a girl's hand, 'told me she's getting married next month when her fiancé returns.'

All the women began to congratulate her and her mother – and, in doing so, tacitly agreed to hide the older girls, regardless of their own safety, so they could not be harmed before their marriage.

Chapter 5

The boys took turns to keep watch at the windows, while the rest sat in front of the fire and ate the grain that two women had found in the kitchen and cooked. It was dark, the sky overcast, hiding the crescent moon, which illuminated the cloud that cast pale light across the snowy fields surrounding the farmhouse.

The boys positioned themselves between the heavy curtains and the window so that the light from the fire didn't reflect on the window and hinder their view. Earlier, one of the men had told them that if the curtains were drawn the room would be warmer, but they knew that in fact the light would attract the attention of troops moving in darkness.

The youngest children fell asleep in their mothers' arms, and the boys who were not on watch tended the fire, as the old men stared into the embers. The four older girls sat together near the fire, nodding off and jerking awake, until they lay down on the floor, their heads on each other's shoulders. At about ten o'clock Otto slid out from behind the curtain and whispered, 'Someone's coming.'

The older girls jumped up and ran to the cupboard at the rear of the house as voices followed by footsteps crossed the porch. Ida pulled Peter to her side. The sound of wood sliding across wood echoed from the back of the house as the girls sealed themselves under the floor. When Ida saw the door handle turn, she coughed loudly to cover the noise. Everybody else sat quietly without looking at each other, as though they were in a doctor's waiting room.

Eight soldiers, including one who had been there earlier, came in. Three were laughing as if they were home from an evening out. One exclaimed, 'Good evening,' in practised German and another commented on the house, '*Warm, gut.*' When nobody replied, a soldier produced a bottle of German wine and held it out as a guest might to his hosts. Again, nobody moved or spoke. The two old men stared at the floor. The children watched the soldiers, while their mothers pretended to adjust their clothing, buttoning up their collars and pulling their coats across their chests.

'Is it already time to leave?' Ida asked, hoping to defuse the situation.

One soldier turned to the others and repeated 'time' and 'leave', apparently trying to interpret.

Ida struggled to remember the Masurian and Polish equivalent: 'Train? Leave?'

Her words startled the men. Then one said, 'Not until tomorrow morning.'

Another asked, 'Have you been to Russia?'

Ida asked him to repeat the question. *Keep them talking*, her father's voice told her.

'Have you visited Russia?' he asked again.

'No,' she said. 'My husband—' then stopped herself and blushed, realising they would know her husband was a soldier. She suddenly feared questions about him, who for all she knew had behaved the same in Russia as Russian soldiers were behaving here. She changed the subject. 'My father. Tannenberg.'

Then she remembered that Poles referred to the battle differently. 'Grunwald,' she added.

'Grunwald?' repeated the soldier.

'Yes,' Ida said. 'Grunwald, Tannenberg. Same.'

A third soldier said, 'Yes, my father in Grunwald, too. Where your father now?'

'Königsberg,' Ida lied. 'Old man. Sick.'

After what seemed like five minutes, but was probably only a few seconds, the same soldier asked, 'Your husband?'

'Paris.' This time Ida lied without hesitation. 'Beautiful city. Like Moscow. Sweets – sends for the children from Paris.'

'Sweets,' Leyna said.

The soldiers laughed.

Ida took a deep breath and tried to think of more to keep them talking, but she could think of nothing but the names of cities. 'Moscow?' Perhaps one lived there.

None replied.

'Minsk?'

Then a man understood what she meant. 'No city. Country. Like East Prussia. Farm,' he said and waved at his comrades. 'From farms.'

Ida glanced at the other women for support – but it was plain that no one knew any Russian. She could see how frightened they were, which only increased her own anxiety.

She switched to a Masurian-Polish: 'Do you speak Polish?'

'A little,' a soldier said.

'Your mother Polish?'

'Russian,' he said. 'Belarusian.'

'Do you have children?' she asked them, in Polish. There was no response, so she said, 'Child?' in Russian.

There was silence. Then a soldier said in German, quietly, 'Two.'

Again the room fell silent.

Ida searched frantically for something more to say. At first she couldn't think of anything, then suddenly remembered a Russian word and said it without thinking: 'Wife?'

None of the soldiers would look at her.

Remembering a second word, Ida quickly added, 'Mother?'

The one near the back who had offered the wine whispered something to the others. Two soldiers left the room, while the others remained. The villagers heard them opening and closing doors. When they returned, they seemed to have reached some agreement. Then one finally said to Ida, 'You. Wife. For tonight.'

The other soldiers laughed nervously.

When Ida said nothing, he said in a stern, flat voice, 'Now!'

As before, she went out without protest. It was the only way to protect the children and the other women. Three soldiers followed her. She heard a soldier in the living room speak, then a woman crying, *'Nein, nein.'*

Ida went into one of the upstairs bedrooms. When she heard the door close behind her she didn't turn round. A few moments later a gunshot made her jump, then another. The children! She could no longer protect them. How many more times would she have to go through this? How many more men? What were they thinking? She felt her mind slip – an almost physical sensation, as if she were sinking into the mattress. She separated her mind from her body. They could have her body, but she would not surrender her mind.

The only way she knew to protect it was to let it set off on its own journey, beyond the room, the house, the peninsula. She took a deep breath, exhaled slowly, letting her mind leave the room. She remembered a holiday near the Mansurian lakes, where her grandparents owned a small cottage. The shrieks in the room below faded as she recalled the scent of the humid air when they had arrived each summer and the warmth of the sun against her skin. She had worn a dress her grandmother had made the week before, in a fabric that matched the flowers blooming along the shore. She and her brother rowed, the oars slipping through the water, propelling the boat, until small waves rocked it gently. A light breeze rippled the surface, carrying with it the scent of the woods. She imagined she was a butterfly, fluttering across the water, rising higher and higher above the lake, her children balancing carefully on her back as they rose with her into the sky, free of the water, the earth and the fires down below.

Chapter 6

When Ida opened her eyes, the muted light of dawn was seeping in through the window. The sun had begun its climb over the peninsula – its globe hidden, however, like the moon the night before, by the overcast sky. The house was as silent as if it had been abandoned. She listened for her children. At first she heard nothing, then the sound of footsteps downstairs. She sat up. The room was empty.

As she stood up to retrieve her dress she felt pain in her lower back, then between her legs. Her neck was sore too, as if somebody had held it tightly. She picked up her coat, which had acted as a pillow, pulled it tightly round her and nervously fastened each button before she stepped out on to the landing. A woman was stretched out on the bed in the next room. She went in to wake her, but when Ida touched her cold skin she knew she was dead. She ran downstairs. In the living room the two old men were sitting in the same chairs. They were very still. There was a small hole in the forehead of one and a trickle of dried blood on his cheek. The other had been shot through the chest.

The fire had gone out.

Women and their children were crouching by the hearth,

shivering. At first, Ida couldn't see hers and panicked. Then she spotted Leyna with the other children. The boys slid out from behind the davenport.

'Where are the girls?'

No one answered.

Holding Leyna's hand, she walked out of the room to the back of the house. The cupboard door was ajar. She went to the windows, glanced out into the field to make sure no one was watching, then returned to the cupboard. It was filled with coats and shoes. Ida searched for the trapdoor, unable to find the seam. After searching further, she found it, then discovered she needed a knife to slip into the crack. She went to the kitchen, found one, then levered it up. Before she had lifted it very far, she was startled by a high-pitched scream. She fell back, dropping both the trapdoor and the knife.

After recovering, she picked up the knife again, slipped it into the crack a second time and repeated the process. This time she didn't let the screams startle her. 'Sh, it's only me.'

The four girls were wrapped in each other's arms, shaking with terror. Ida reached in to help them out but they shrank back. Then, realising she was holding the knife above them, she put it down and reached in again. 'I need your help.'

As they were climbing out, they froze. Footsteps rounded the hall.

A woman, wearing a wet coat, entered the room. 'Where's my daughter?'

Ida pointed at the cupboard, as another girl's mother appeared.

'Where were you?' she asked the woman in the wet coat.

'We hid in the forest last night. We ran when the soldier guarding us chased one of the boys into the kitchen.'

Ida gestured at the coats in the cupboard. 'They're dry,' she said. 'Take one. We must go.'

When everyone had gathered in the living room, Ida stepped towards the door to initiate movement. A young girl grabbed Peter's hand. When the girl's mother saw her holding Peter's hand she stood up, walked over and held her daughter's free hand, while the rest of the group assembled.

The party set off towards the crossroads at Weidehnen. They had walked only a kilometre when they saw the commissar in the sleigh. He was alone but at the sight of his Russian uniform panic erupted. A girl ran into the snow-filled ditch at the side of the road, while a woman turned and began to run back towards where they had come from.

'Don't run!' Ida called.

She fled anyway, but Ida persuaded the girl to come out of the ditch.

The commissar slowed his horse. '*Guten Morgen*,' he called. 'Is everything all right?'

'Yes.'

'Where are the others?'

Ida didn't reply.

'The truck is waiting up the road at Weidehnen,' he went on. 'They'll take you to the station for evacuation.' He pointed to the woman who was running up the road. 'I'll try to convince her to go with you. What's her name?'

'Irmgard,' someone said.

'Irmgard,' he repeated, then slapped the reins on the horses' backs and moved on.

The women and children trudged on. Within two kilometres they were passing dead German soldiers again, at first scattered in ones and twos, then, a kilometre further on, a heap near the road, apparently for transport to a mass grave. The Russians would have to bury the dead, if only to curb the spread of disease.

When they came within sight of Dirschkein, the last settlement before Weidehnen, Ida told the others that she and her children were turning off. 'Follow us if you wish,' she said. 'But we must move fast.'

'Won't it be safer in Weidehnen?' a woman asked.

'He said they'd take us to a train,' another added.

'For evacuation.'

'Their trains don't go west,' Ida said.

'You said earlier we should go east.'

'Not by train, though. It'll take us too far.'

There was a moment of confusion. Ida stepped back, as the women bickered.

'He said Weidehnen would be safe.'

'They can't be trusted. Look what's already happened!'

'The officer in the sleigh seems honest.'

'Not everyone can be bad,' the oldest said. 'Anyway, I'm tired. I can't walk for ever.'

The women argued back and forth until Ida said, 'Don't go. They'll take you to Russia.'

'We don't need a whore telling us what to do!' snapped the mother of a teenage girl.

For a moment Ida was stunned. Then, without acknowledging what had been said, she took Leyna's hand and went towards the forest with the three children. The women let her go, still arguing among themselves.

When the family entered the forest, Ida heard one of the mothers shout something. It was too late. Otto, finding himself at the front, instinctively led the family deeper into the trees. He saw a willow and snapped off a thin branch as he passed, holding it tightly in his hand. When they reached the first fork in the path on which they had entered the forest, Peter passed Otto and veered to the left as he began to push the pace, forcing Ida and Leyna to fall in line.

Chapter 7

'We'll go to Thierenberg,' Ida said, after they had stopped to rest half an hour later.

As they passed on through the forest, they heard fighting to the west, towards Germau. Like the previous morning when the Russian troops had entered Germau, the explosions occasionally grew louder, moving in their direction, before receding.

After a particularly heavy round of distant artillery fire the forest fell completely silent. Ida remembered the warm rolls she had placed on the kitchen table the previous morning, which they had had no chance to eat. She thought of her father and of Karl. To distract herself from what might have been their fate, she began to count in Latin, '*Unus, duo, tres, quattuor, quinque, sex, septem, octo—*' she broke off – shocked by more shelling.

'What are you talking about?' Leyna asked.

'Leave her alone,' Peter said.

Ida picked Leyna up and kissed her, then put her down, but as soon as her feet touched the ground she started to cry.

'Shut up!' Peter yelled, which made her cry all the more.

Ida picked her up again to comfort her, and they walked on through the undergrowth, until they were at the edge of a large clearing. Once they were convinced that no one was around, they crossed the field and re-entered the forest. They struggled through thick brush for a while and reached another clearing. 'I think that's the road ahead,' Peter said.

Ida sent the boys to see if any soldiers were about. While they were gone, Leyna began to complain about hunger. The boys soon returned to report that the road was clear as far as they could tell. On the road, Ida heard her father's voice again: *Stay by the edge, away from the cobbles. If anyone approaches, you have to see them first.*

They settled into a brisk pace, walking in single file. Otto, at the rear, kept turning round fully to check that no one was behind them. Suddenly Peter stopped. 'Something's ahead.'

They dived into the brush at the side of the road. Ida was praying, as they lay, hardly daring to breathe. The sun was high overhead behind thick cloud, but the air was chilly. After a while, Ida told Peter to creep out and see what was going on.

When he came back he told her he could still see something, he didn't know what, but that nothing was moving. Ida joined him and saw the silhouette of a vehicle with what appeared to be a man sitting on the bonnet and others on the ground nearby.

They climbed back into the bushes to hide. Fleeing, Ida thought, was as much about the art of concealment as it was about covering ground. Half an hour later Ida told Peter to look again. When he got back, it was only to report that nothing had changed. Ida knew that the vehicle was parked at the entrance to the road leading to Thierenberg. She told the children they would go on, still at the edge of the road, but they must be ready to hide at her command. This time she took the lead, her eyes fixed on the motionless figures ahead. As they neared the vehicle she saw three men lying face down. The man sitting on the bonnet was hunched over another, whose body held him in an upright position.

The closer they moved to the junction, the more bodies they saw. Ida told the children to move to the middle of the road to avoid the bodies – of young Russian soldiers this time. They appeared to have died that day, the first Russian casualties the family had seen.

Ida decided it was too dangerous to go into Thierenberg and moved back into the forest, Leyna clasping her hand. Ida glanced down at her, then at Peter and Otto. *God help me.* Two or three kilometres to the east there was a hamlet where three farmers lived – Paul had bought livestock from them to slaughter for the shop. 'We'll try Auerhof,' she said.

She tried to remember the location of the path that led there, then decided simply to walk east. They would soon reach the pastures in which the farmers worked during the summer. The journey was longer than she had expected, probably because she had never gone to the farm through the forest in winter before. Soon, however, the fields appeared and in the distance she could see the three farmhouses. Beyond the houses on the barn roofs were stork's nests covered with snow and she wished she could fly away to Africa and the warmth of the south.

They no longer formed a neat, single-file line. The four moved in disarray – tired and hunched, not caring whether someone might see them. They were in the open now, with no escape route.

'Maybe one of the farmers is still here,' Ida said, to raise the children's spirits.

'There's no smoke from the chimneys,' Peter said.

'They'll be hiding.'

Halfway across the pasture she listened for livestock, but all was silent. When they reached the first house Peter ran to the porch to peer through the windows.

'No one's here.'

'Knock on the door.'

No one came.

Ida told him to try the door.

It was unlocked.

Cautiously they entered the house. The hardwood floors amplified the sound of their footsteps. The furniture was undisturbed, as the owners had originally arranged it. In the dining room the table had been laid with napkins, plates, knives, forks, spoons, cups and saucers.

'Try upstairs,' Ida told the boys. 'Someone must be about.'

They soon returned with the news that the house was empty.

'Go to the neighbours' houses.'

While Ida and Leyna waited on the porch, the boys did as she had asked.

A few minutes later they were back: no one was about. The undisturbed houses frightened Ida more than if they had been ransacked. The quiet and order of the hamlet sent a chill through her. Had they walked into a trap? Were they being lulled by a false sense of security? She searched the snow for tracks, trying to calm herself. She couldn't think clearly because she was tired, she told herself. Her father had warned her of this – it was at such times that fatal errors of judgement occurred. The memory of the rapes surged in, the pain, the humiliation, almost overwhelming her.

Without looking down, she became aware that Peter was staring at her and felt bitter shame that he knew what the soldiers had done to her. She took a deep breath, ran her hand through his hair and focused on survival. They needed shelter and food. She met Peter's eyes. 'Let's see if we can find something to eat,' she said.

They went back into the first house and Ida entered the kitchen. She found bottled fruit and vegetables in the pantry, with some salt pork. 'We won't make a fire,' she said. 'Somebody might see the smoke.'

'How will we keep warm?'

'We'll look for blankets after we've eaten.'

She put vegetables and fruit on to each plate, then some pork.

They stayed in the kitchen and ate in silence. When they had washed the plates and put them away, they went upstairs to find blankets. Each bed was perfectly made, as though the owner had been expecting guests. Otto began to pull the blankets off a bed, but Ida stopped him. 'Don't disturb it. There should be others somewhere.'

Peter called that he had found extra blankets in the cupboard at the top of the stairs. Ida removed only as many as they needed. 'We won't stay in the house,' she said. 'We'll hide in the barn.'

'But they'll find us,' Peter said.

'Maybe not. There's plenty in the houses to keep them busy.'

They went outside and Ida led them away from the barn into the woods.

'Where are we going?' Otto asked, pointing in the opposite direction. 'The barn's back there.'

'We'll come back through the woods, without leaving tracks from the house.'

The forest canopy kept the snow off the forest floor, allowing them to cross the woods to the barn, whose back abutted the trees, without leaving tracks. Inside, they climbed a ladder to the loft and pulled it up behind them. As Ida had hoped, the space was covered with a thick bed of straw. She made a nest in it, then lined it with blankets. After gathering on top of them, they pulled the others over them and covered themselves with straw. The air trapped inside quickly warmed.

Safe at last, everyone lay still, glad to be out of the cold. Soon the children were whispering to each other. When Ida asked what they were talking about, they began to sing very softly, 'Happy Birthday to you . . .'

Peter had remembered her birthday in spite of all they had gone through.

When they had finished he asked, 'What would you like for a present?'

'Tell us!' Otto whispered, almost excited.

Ida paused, then murmured, 'German soldiers,' and added, 'Alive.'

When they woke in the morning the clearing was as silent as it had been the night before. Otto pushed the blankets away from their heads and they lay on their backs, gazing up at the rafters.

'We'll stay here today,' Ida said, 'and make a plan for tomorrow. We can take turns to watch, but if anyone has to go outside, you must stay in the woods.'

'Grandpa said to keep moving,' Peter said.

'Leyna needs to rest – we all do.'

They remained in the straw bed through the early part of morning, making up songs, while Otto and Peter took turns peeking through a crack in the roof.

'There's an elk in the field.'

Everyone crawled over to take turns admiring it through the crack.

'We should go and get some food,' Ida said, 'but we'd better be more careful than we were yesterday. Only one of us will go into the house – we've already left too many marks.'

'I'll go,' Peter said.

'No, I will. If something happens, you will have to get everyone to Pillau.'

'But, Mutti—'

'It's important. If you see someone come when I'm in the house, stay here and keep quiet. Don't worry about me. I'll catch up with you.'

Leyna began to cry. Ida pulled her into her arms. 'Nothing will happen to me,' she whispered. Then she told Otto and Peter that if something did they were to go south along the road to Thierenberg until they reached a junction at which they would head west. 'Eventually you'll reach Fischhausen. Someone there will take you to Pillau. Ships are waiting there to take you west.' She turned back to Leyna. 'We'll be together, but it's always best to make plans.' She put the child down and stood up. 'When I'm downstairs, knock twice on the floor if the field is empty.' She climbed down the ladder, went to the door facing the forest and waited for the signal.

The house was as immaculate as it had been previously, but the cleanliness still made her uneasy. It seemed too neat. She wondered again if someone was hiding upstairs . . . 'Stop it,' she said aloud.

She entered the pantry and took some meat, and four bottles of fruit and vegetables. She put the meat on the work surface, cut some thin slices, laid them on a plate, then returned the joint to the pantry.

She gathered everything on a cloth and pulled the four corners together into a makeshift sack. Then she peered out of the dining-room window across the empty meadow and checked the other side of the house, before hurrying out of the front door and into the forest.

A few minutes later she entered the barn.

Chapter 8

After hiding in the loft the remainder of the afternoon, the boys grew restless.

'Can we go outside?' Otto asked.

'It's too early. Wait until sunset,' Ida said.

'If it's dark we might not find our way back,' Peter said.

He was right, she thought. 'Go on, then, but stay together. And *don't* get lost.'

Peter and Otto climbed down the ladder and slipped out of the barn's rear door. At first they searched for a path that would take them to the road in the morning, as Ida had asked them to, but the search soon degenerated into a game of tag, as the boys burned off the excess energy they had stored up hiding. They chased each other through the trees until they were out of breath.

They flopped on to the ground and lay there, panting, until they heard a distant sound. They held their breath and listened.

'Did you hear that?'

'I don't know.'

They got to their feet and followed the sound deeper into the forest, until they reached a frozen bog. They crossed the ice, then started up a hill. Every few minutes they stopped to memorise landmarks, so that they would be able to find their way back. At the top of the hill they reached the edge of the forest and hid behind a tree to look out across an open field, covered with snow, which seemed to go on for ever, broken only by an occasional copse. It reminded Peter of the dunes that stretched the length of the Curonian Spit – the strip of land that shielded the Curonian Lagoon from the Baltic a short distance north where his family had gone with their father when he had visited.

'What's that?' Otto asked, interrupting Peter's thoughts. He was pointing towards the horizon. 'Over there.' Peter peered across the hills, then focused on the horizon, where the last swell fell away to oblivion.

'Further left,' Otto said. 'Just below the rise.'

Peter squinted. Then he saw it – so clearly that he was surprised he had missed it before. They looked like toys in the distance. 'Panzers,' he said, studying the outline. 'They're ours.'

A line of five tanks drove slowly down the rise, followed by a few artillery vehicles and several horse-drawn cannons. The panzer had been Karl's and Peter's favourite vehicle since they had both seen them parked in a long row on the outskirts of Königsberg years earlier. Convinced they weren't Russian T-38s, he walked out from behind the tree to stand in the open.

'What are you doing? They'll see you.'

'They're German, stupid. It doesn't matter.'

Suddenly the boys remembered Ida's birthday wish. They sprinted into the forest as fast as they could, without stopping to check for their landmarks. They tore down the hill, racing on until they saw an opening through the trees and burst into the field where the houses stood. They ran straight across the middle to the barn, without pausing to make sure no one was about, leaving clear tracks to their hiding place. When they reached the barn, they slipped through the back door and shouted, 'Germans!'

Ida's head appeared from the loft.

'They're here!' Peter shouted.

'Alive!' Otto added.

'Come up here,' she said and slid the ladder down.

'We saw them,' Peter said, as he climbed the rungs and fell into the straw.

'Over there,' Otto said, pointing in the direction they had come from.

'How far?'

'Through the woods. A few hills away.'

She listened to the boys' excited voices and tried to calculate where the battalion was headed. She assumed they were planning to attack the Russian troops in Germau, but she didn't know where other Russian forces might be concentrated on the peninsula.

'Are you sure they're heading towards us?' she asked the boys again. 'I need to know exactly what you saw.'

The boys repeated their story.

'So, they'll probably come down the road north of us. It's the only one that leads west,' Ida said. 'I'll try to meet them and see if they'll take us with them.'

'Let me and Otto go.'

'I need you to stay here and take care of Leyna.' They had to be ready to go quickly if she convinced the soldiers to take them.

She didn't want to stand out on the road, in case Russian scouts were in the area, so she waited inside, hoping to catch the convoy just before it passed. Even though dusk would not fall for another hour she buttoned her coat and smoothed the front, then ran her fingers through her hair in a bid to make herself presentable. She was imagining herself and the children in Berlin, safe from the combat surrounding them, but stopped herself, realising her request might be rebuffed by the soldiers.

An hour later they heard a soft rumbling in the distance, little more than a vibration, like wind in the trees. A few minutes passed as Ida worked up the courage to go. 'Wait for me here,' she said to the boys. Then she leaned down, kissed Leyna and whispered, 'Do as Peter tells you.'

She looked straight at Peter, her silent way of telling him to take care of everybody if anything unexpected occurred. He broke eye contact and glanced down at the straw. Ida stood up, walked to the edge of the loft and disappeared down the ladder. She had paid little attention to the crisp air until she stepped out into the clearing. Now she could hear the vehicles clearly. She walked towards the road, passing the three houses, and entered the forest. It ran parallel to the one they had walked along the day before. She knew that if she continued in a straight line through the forest, she would eventually come to it. It occurred to her that she had never before ventured into the forest alone at night and she was reminded of the stories she had been told during childhood about the ancient invaders on horseback; the soldiers she was in search of were descendants of the tribe who had conquered the peninsula seven centuries earlier. Now she hoped they would rescue her and the children.

She was standing in the middle of the road – she'd been so deep in thought that she hadn't noticed she was leaving the forest behind – and could hear diesel engines and metal tracks clanking against the cobbled road engulfing the dark night, until the sound grew so loud that she worried that she might be swallowed by the noise itself.

The road was flat for some three hundred metres, then climbed over a small rise. As the first tank slammed over the hill she shrank back in terror – it was so vast against the darkened sky, the noise almost deafening. It occurred to her that she might have made a grave mistake. It looked like an enormous black metal thunderhead as it rolled down the hill towards her. She pressed her left hand over the top of her right to keep it from trembling and reached into her coat pocket for the white cloth in which she had carried the food as the second tank came into view. She could see the outline of a soldier sitting on the first, bearing down on her.

As it came close enough, she saw a small flag with a hand-drawn swastika draped over the front. She raised the white cloth as high as she could and stepped to the edge of the road, squeezing her eyes shut, as though that might help to shut out the roar. And, in fact, the noise died, replaced by the rumble of idling engines and a strong smell of diesel. She soon heard voices – speaking German. Someone asked her to identify herself.

At first she didn't understand what they wanted, then realised they wanted to know if she was German – German as well as Christian. Before she could answer, three or four men, maybe more – numbers were losing meaning – surrounded her and told her to go to a jeep further down the convoy. Halfway there a hand brushed her hips. At first she tried to ignore it, but when a second touched she whipped round. 'I'm German, for God's sake!'

The soldiers paused, but only briefly. 'Well, of course. So are we,' one said.

'I need your help,' Ida said.

'Perhaps you can help us too.'

A hand slipped under her coat. She paused and tried to retreat, but her pause was interpreted as willingness, for no sooner had she pulled back than she felt another hand undoing the buttons, sliding across her breasts, sliding downwards. She was forced to the ground.

Instead of trying to blank it out, as she had before, she told herself to remain as lucid as possible, as though preserving her memories were the only power she retained, memories she would one day use to avenge herself on the men assaulting her – if it took a year, a decade, a lifetime, half a century. She would never forgive the Russian soldiers for what they had done and even less these Germans, because they were supposed to be her own. She prayed that their actions now would haunt them for ever.

The fourth or fifth man to force himself on her was interrupted by the sound of a horse-drawn wagon approaching. Ida heard someone step down to the ground and walk towards her. The men stood to attention and yanked her back to her feet. The officer glanced round, then, without reprimanding them or asking questions, he told Ida to join him in his vehicle. At first she thought it was a cruel joke, but she turned and followed him, secure in her decision to pass on, one day, the details of her rescue.

Chapter 9

Peter, Otto and Leyna sat in the loft listening to the tanks crossing the forest. The noise was so loud that they expected them to appear in the middle of the field in front of the barn. But just when it seemed they might smash through the wall, the engines calmed to an idle and became indiscernible from the breeze that started blowing through the trees.

They sat in the straw as the wind pushed through the cracks between the boards, creating a muted whistling, as though calling them outside. A chill entered the room. Leyna leaned close to her brother. Every few minutes they felt sure they could hear Ida running through the forest, but, listening more closely, they realised it was only the wind.

It was dark now so they could no longer mark the passage of time. At first, after Ida had left, Peter had been able to guess that a quarter of an hour had passed, then half an hour, from the darkening sky. Now he was no longer sure whether she had been gone forty-five minutes or two hours.

At long last they heard something outside: someone was running in their direction. The barn's rear door swung open.

'Mutti?' Leyna called.

Peter clasped his hand over her mouth. There was a moment

of silence, as though whoever was below was listening for them as well.

'They're coming,' Ida answered. 'Part of the group will spend the night here.'

Peter gave a sigh of relief.

In the distance he could hear the panzer engines rumbling back to life as they moved up the road, but away from them. Instead, horses' hooves were clopping towards the barn.

'Why were you so long?' he asked.

Ida didn't answer his question. 'You can come down now. I promised to show them where the food is.'

The sound of horses was more distinct now. When Peter stepped out of the barn, he saw a six-horse team pulling the first of three double-axle cannons into view. Two men appeared on horseback, then a single-axle cart pulled by two horses arrived. Later Peter discovered that it was a 'goulash cannon', a giant cooking vat into which the soldiers threw any food they found – potatoes, carrots, meat, flour, water, part of an elk that one of the tanks had run over three days earlier, with some wild boar that one of the soldiers had shot. All the supply lines had been severed so the troops had to forage. The cook boiled everything into a stew, then served it to the men.

It was still early in the evening, but the ghostly clearing and the three abandoned houses were bustling with life. The soldiers lit small fires, apparently unconcerned about the arrival of Russian troops. An officer stood in the middle of the activity, shouting orders, as though mayor of a newly settled hamlet.

By then Peter, Otto and Leyna were on a porch watching the soldiers searching about for places to sleep. Ida ran up and down the stairs of the largest house, showing an officer, with whom she seemed unusually friendly, the food caches in the house, as two soldiers carried it out of the house to the goulash cannon. Three more disappeared into the barn and emerged with armfuls of hay for the horses.

An hour or so later the soldiers were still running about, mending cannon trailers and cleaning their rifles. Then another group of men moved out of the forest near the barn and into the light cast by the fires. The officer shouted orders as the soldiers grabbed their rifles and dropped to their stomachs in the snow.

'Volkssturm! Don't shoot!'

Within minutes, the newcomers had been disarmed and marched to the centre of the clearing for questioning.

Peter didn't know any of them by name, but he could see from their features that they were natives of the peninsula: their faces were gaunt, their mouths thinner and their eyes deeper set than those of the other troops. They seemed to Peter to have little in common with the German army surrounding them. Eventually Ida asked the officer to stop interrogating them. 'Can't you see that they need food? They know the area better than your men do. When they're warm and fed they might be of help.'

The officer frowned, but what she said must have made sense to him because he stalked away, leaving her alone with them.

'Where are you from?' she asked.

Without speaking, one gestured to a house in the clearing. 'Thierenberg,' said another.

'I'm from Germau,' Ida said, 'those are my children.' She waved to them on the porch. 'You must be hungry,' she added.

'*Ja* – and need fresh clothes.' He began to move towards his house. Ida followed him with the others. 'When you're ready, I'll have a hot meal for you.' They nodded and disappeared into the man's home.

Chapter 10

Later, the men sat at the dining table, drawing diagrams of the peninsula. For the moment the officer treated them as his peers – Ida had been right about their familiarity with the immediate area. Peter and Otto were still on the porch, watching the soldiers. The two who had arrived on horseback earlier were woken around midnight – they had gone to sleep in the middle house. With their horses now fed and rested, they prepared to mount.

'Where are they going?' Otto asked the man nearest him.

'To find out if the road is clear for us to travel tomorrow.'

Ida appeared behind the boys. 'What are you up to?' she asked.

'Keeping watch.'

'Well, it's time for bed.'

As Otto went into the house with his aunt, he thought about his mother in Berlin and wondered, suddenly homesick, whether she was safe. At least Peter and Leyna had their mother with them. Would he ever see his again? He lay down with Peter in the corner of the dining room, beside the sleeping Leyna, certain that he would be awake all night, worrying about Elsa, but as soon as he closed his eyes he was asleep.

Later that night Peter woke with a start. The room was dark

when he opened his eyes but through the gloom he made out his mother's figure with an officer. They tiptoed out, closing the door softly behind them. Where was she going? His heart sank as it occurred to him that she must have made a deal with him. He lay waiting her return. When he became too sleepy to keep his eyes open any longer, he closed them and drifted off.

A few hours later he awoke again to the sound of men's voices outside. He reached for his mother, but she was not there. He listened. At first two or three men were talking together, then others joined them. He heard the heavy body of a horse shuffling around.

Within five or ten minutes the soldiers had moved away from the house; a man shouted orders. Then Peter heard boots walking across the floor above him. It was still dark – even darker than it had been earlier since the lanterns had been put out and the fires had burned low.

The door opened and someone came in. His mother. He felt her lean down to slide her hand over Leyna's cheek, then she shook Otto's arm.

'Up you get. It's almost time to leave.'

'Where are we going?' Otto asked.

'With the soldiers.'

The children pulled on their coats. When they went out into the cold, dark yard, the first team of horses was harnessed to the lead cannon. A group of soldiers was readying the others.

In the far distance they could hear the rumbling of shells fired, a sound that had been constant for days before the Russian soldiers had taken Germau. So familiar had the artillery accompaniment become that they worried only when it stopped. There were too many opposing forces on the peninsula by then for such calm. Silence meant that troops were on the move – and the family had no idea whom they might run into or where.

The two scouts had returned at around three o'clock from reconnaissance in line with the Volkssturm's directions. They had found a German battalion separated from their regiment in battle the previous week near Insterburg. Their commanding officer had said that a Russian regiment was encamped nearby and might be surrounded if the group in Auerhof joined his.

As Ida stood on the porch with the children, a soldier pointed to the goulash cannon at the rear of the column. 'There's room for you on top,' he said to the children. 'Your mother can sit here.' He patted the seat beside him on the lead cannon wagon. 'What about my little girl?' Ida asked, picking up Leyna.

'Bring her with you.'

She bent down to Peter and Otto. 'It's only for a little while,' she reassured them.

As she walked to the front of the line, she passed some soldiers studying a map. 'Which village did you say you were from?' one asked.

'Germau.'

'Where is it?'

She took the map, found the coastal town of Palmnicken and followed the road inland to her home. 'Here,' she said.

'How many soldiers?'

'I don't know.'

'Panzers?'

'I didn't see any. Ask the boys.'

Two men walked to where the boys were seated on the goulash cannon. They asked them what they had seen in Germau, then about their journey across the peninsula and the night they had spent at the house. They wanted to know exactly what the Russians had done and how many soldiers they had seen – alive, dead, German or Russian. But the only thing either child could remember with clarity was that they had seen seventeen dead horses. They had kept count to distract themselves from the rest of the carnage. The men weren't interested in dead horses: 'Which way were the soldiers moving?'

'To Germau,' Peter replied.

Chapter 11

Thirty minutes later the column started out into the night, towards the road where Ida had first encountered them. After reaching it and turning left towards Thierenberg, they travelled without incident until a bright flare lit up the sky directly overhead, turning the moonless night to day. They stopped. Another flare shot up and exploded. Peter watched the horses' breath in the cold air, like tiny puffs of fog floating in from the sea. The battalion was still deep in the forest so the officer in charge decided that, although they had been caught in the light, they had probably not been seen, shielded as they were by the trees. He ordered the company forward.

Soon they came to the main crossroads before Thierenberg. Ahead, above the trees, they could see the orange glow of fire. The column halted again. The only sound was of flames crackling and snapping, no gunfire. The line lurched forward, towards the fires licking clean the interior of buildings, lighting the cobbled road as it cut through the trees. They passed the remnants of houses reduced to smouldering ash that glowed yellow and red in the dark.

A few minutes later, when they entered the square, every house in the village was ablaze; there was no sign of life. Ida glanced back automatically to check that the boys were safe, but she was not thinking about the children. Her aunt and uncle had lived in this village. She hadn't seen them often, but they had always treated her as if she were one of their own children. She looked across to the church, whose steeple still towered above the village, if not for much longer: it, too, was being consumed by the flames. There was little chance that anyone was hiding in the church now. In any case, she knew she could not persuade the soldiers to stop while she searched – the heat was so intense that they would not leave the road.

Eventually they turned into a field at the end of the village. The destruction they had just witnessed silenced everyone. Peter sensed the soldiers' mood: it reminded him of his father when he had been confronted with something he didn't want to do. He suddenly wondered where his father was. They had not heard that he was dead, but they had no idea now where he might be.

His grandfather, he thought, would be pacing around his house, trying to picture the battles being fought across the peninsula and guessing where his daughter and grandchildren were. Ever since the Great War had ended he had studied war tactics and strategies, although he was too old and infirm to fight. Landwirt had expressed no fear during the weeks before the front had reached them. Even on the morning that Ida had sent him back to Sorgenau, so that he wouldn't be caught and killed either in Germau or on the way home, he had been more irritated than frightened. Suddenly Peter saw how like her father his mother was; she didn't have his interest in war, but she stayed calm. She knew she couldn't control what happened to them, so she didn't worry about terrifying possibilities. Instead, she focused on planning their next move.

Peter no longer wanted to think about the dangers that lay ahead either, so he concentrated on the rhythmic clatter of the horses' hooves, as the patient beasts hauled the wagons across the icy field, their heavy breathing and the sound of their lips vibrating as they exhaled.

Otto was examining his surroundings. Parts of the peninsula were still new to him, although he had lived there now for more than a year. 'Where are we going?' he asked the driver.

The reply was drowned by another burst of flares overhead, then heavy artillery fire pounded the ground around them. 'Stalin's organ,' the driver muttered, as a burst of Katyusha rockets cut through the air from a series of hidden cannons mounted on the back of a truck – a weapon every German soldier on the Eastern Front had grown to dread – but even as the shells rained on them, bursts of light exposing their positions, they continued to move at the same pace. As the fire became heavier, a scout on horseback rode down the line, relaying the commanding officer's orders not to alter direction or speed but to split. The line divided cleanly into a 'Y' shape, then readjusted back into parallel lines.

The guns fell silent. Neither German line could return fire: doing so would require that they stop and set up in their exposed position, which would provide the enemy with a chance to pinpoint their coordinates for a direct hit. A strange tranquillity settled over the group. Soldiers were piled into the cart with the children. At that moment their faces showed neither fear nor anger – not even desire for revenge, only survival. They knew their safety lay with fate and that no one could predict the outcome, but they were prepared: they would fight. A light flashed on the horizon and the soldiers shifted nervously in their seats. It came again, followed by a series of fiery tails; the crisp whoosh of missiles sliced through the air. The lines split again, each vehicle choosing its own route in an attempt to reduce the odds of being hit.

Like miniature meteorites slamming into the earth, explosions cratered the landscape so violently that the boys clung to their seat as clumps of dirt showered them, the gritty earth finding its way into their mouths. The sky was a mixture of detonating rockets and flares that hung over them like dying stars. On the other side of a field ran a line of trees.

The soldiers, concerned only with reaching cover, ignored the explosions – their horses, just as intent, ran straight ahead. At last the splintered battalion eased past the trees – to discover that the third cannon, with its operators, had been hit. The survivors paused briefly, in memory, then reassembled into a single line, hidden by the overhanging trees, and began to move south.

Chapter 12

In the forest artillery fire grew louder as they pressed deeper among the trees, the horses struggling to maintain their momentum. When they reached a crossroads the officer ordered his men into position along the opposite side of the intersecting road, which was narrow and overgrown. The artillery pieces were placed along the shoulder, their bases secured against the ground, their barrels aimed into the woodland.

Ida and the children were sent to the other side of the road and told to hide behind a supply cart as the soldiers fortified their position.

The Russians continued to fire, although their shells were now directed at another battalion that blocked their escape to the rear. The splintered battalions and regiments of the division slowly re-established contact with each other and positioned themselves to box the Russians into their hiding place.

Exhilarated by the events unfolding around them, Peter and Otto watched with little apparent fear as the men prepared for battle. Everyone moved with purpose, but there was no sense of frantic rush. Were it not for the explosions in the distance, a passing stranger might have thought the soldiers were getting ready to demonstrate their equipment, rather than engage in a battle.

The sense of workaday ritual was shattered when a series of random salvos from the enemy found the line. A volley of fire ruptured the forest, followed by a short silence, as if the Russians were trying to work out whether or not they had hit their invisible target. Then another barrage hammered through the trees, louder and more violent than any the family had yet experienced. A supply cart exploded. The soldiers fired back blindly into the forest, their façade of calm turning to panic. They had been caught off guard by the unexpected offensive. One ran, ducking, across the road to where Ida and the children were hidden.

'Go back through there!' He gestured into the forest behind them. 'Don't stop!'

Peter had heard dozens of his grandfather's stories and he realised that the men would soon be engaged in hand-to-hand combat. The Russians would come crashing through the forest, trying to escape the line firing on their rear. Now, as they started running, Peter felt a jolt of fear. He saw the others following as best they could, Ida stopping only long enough to make sure Leyna kept pace.

The barrage was so savage that the ground shook beneath their feet. When it seemed the intensity of fire had reached its apex, the noise shot up even higher, creating an almost physical wall of sound. Just as suddenly it levelled off momentarily, then ceased before the Germans unleashed their own fury. The family had stopped to crouch after running only fifty metres into the trees. They smelled burning rubber, mixed with something they couldn't identify.

In a lull, they began to run again. Leyna was screaming with fright, tripping and falling, so Ida scooped her up and raced after the boys. She didn't care how far they had to run. She would run all night and the next day if she had to.

Chapter 13

The gunfire moved further into the distance now as they forced themselves into darkness beneath the canopy. The undergrowth was so thick that they had to hold out their arms to stop branches and brambles swiping their faces. As the storm of artillery retreated, the darkness became so complete that even a single step forward proved hazardous. Otto rubbed a bump on his forehead – he had run into a tree – and they all held hands in a chain.

A few minutes later they heard ice splintering. They had ventured out from the trees on to a frozen marshland, whose surface had been split by a stray missile. Peter led them along the edge, where the ice was still intact. They went back into the forest and wove a path through the trees, branches and brush that blocked them at every turn. When they had been creeping forward blindly for hours, Ida suggested they rest until dawn. They sat down, huddled together for warmth and remained there until they could see their bootlaces as the first trace of dawn bled into the sky.

In the distance they could still hear the soft rumble of explosions. They tried to decide from where the sound was travelling, then turned and walked in the opposite direction. When they came to a clearing, Otto saw a patch of blue in the otherwise overcast sky. An hour later they heard an engine, then another vehicle approaching. They waited for the sound to fade and continued towards the road.

Soon they caught sight of the edge of the road raised above the forest floor to keep it from flooding in the spring, when the ice melted and turned the area into a swamp. They hid in the brush and waited for another vehicle to go past. As they peered through the branches, they saw a truck coming, with another behind it. When the first was level with them, they saw a black cross outlined in white on the door and again on the second.

'Let's get on to the road before the next one comes,' Peter said.

Almost immediately a lone truck appeared. The driver slowed and waved them to the back, where another soldier pulled them inside. The truck set off, while Otto was still half outside. Ida scrabbled for his other hand and helped the soldier to heave him in. At that moment she glanced out and saw that they were a few kilometres south of Germau on the road to Fischhausen. She and the children had spent the last five days travelling in a circle and were almost back where they had started. The soldier beside her noticed her expression and asked if she was all right. Ida sighed. 'What's happening at Germau?' she asked.

'We took it back, but the Russians recaptured it the next day. Last night we finally pushed them out. Now we wait for their counter-attack,' he said.

They fell silent. The truck's momentum and the soldier nearby provided enough security for Ida briefly to rest her eyes. A few moments later Leyna tugged at her sleeve. 'Look, Mutti. There's an aeroplane up in the sky.'

Ida, the soldier and the boys looked out in the direction she was pointing. A plane was flying east across the peninsula from the Baltic. Suddenly it swooped back. It made a wide arc, lined itself up with the road and began its descent from above. Its machine-guns opened up, strafing the road, sending fragments of rock flying into the air, clinking off the truck's metal. Ida and the children ducked, even though there was no cover on the truck. Mercifully, the linden trees that lined the road offered patchy shelter as they entered a verdant tunnel of overhanging branches shielding the road from the sky.

As quickly as it had dived, the plane pulled back up and swept over them. They waited for it to circle and come back to try again, but it flew south towards Fischhausen. Utterly exhausted, the family shrugged off their narrow escape and watched the trees zipping past beside the road they had once travelled along each month on their way to Königsberg to shop at the big market and to visit Ida's parents. A few kilometres north of Fischhausen the truck stopped at a junction.

'The town's not far away now. You should be able to get to Pillau from there,' the driver said, unaware that Ida knew the region better than he did.

After they had jumped down, the truck turned on to a farm track, sped across a field, before disappearing into a stand of trees. The family began to walk down the road. As they neared the top of a hill, they spotted the brick water tower to the north of Fischhausen above the trees. On their journeys to Landwirt's home it had been a familiar landmark, which had broken the monotony of the drive. Now the sight of it produced a sense of calm in Peter that he had not felt since they had fled Germau.

The road ahead was empty. No more trucks passed and they could hear none of the sounds they had grown accustomed to – the roar of engines, gunfire or bombing. It was as though all human activity had ceased, leaving the peninsula deserted but for the livestock that wandered across the road ahead, bellowing, in search of their owners.

Chapter 14

When they got to the water tower, Ida told Peter to climb to the top and look for trucks headed towards Pillau. As he started up the iron rungs, cemented between the bricks, she called after him, 'Be careful,' her voice echoing in the cavernous dark space.

Peter went on up the narrow circular shaft towards the light far above him. He took one step at a time, holding on tightly to the rung above. He was sure he wouldn't fall, but he couldn't help knowing that if he did it was a long way down. He paused, clung to the ladder and rested a moment. He had dreamed of climbing the tower almost since he had first set eyes on it, but he had never thought to have the chance – especially in such circumstances as these. He wished his father were there to see him emerge at the top.

When he reached the portal, he took another deep breath and pushed his head through the opening into the bright sky. He glanced down to make sure his mother was watching and waved, then pulled himself on to the little platform.

Standing there, holding tight to the iron railing circling it, he noticed something on the periphery of his vision. At first he thought his eyes were playing tricks on him. He squeezed them shut and opened them again, but the endless column of people was still there. He had never seen so many in his life, had had no idea so many lived in East Prussia.

A line of people three or four abreast stretched out along the road through Fischhausen towards Pillau as far as he could see. Towards the capital, the column reached to the horizon. From his vantage point it seemed hardly to move. Alongside it lay discarded luggage, boxes, carts and carriages.

'Can you see any trucks?' Ida shouted.

Peter peered down at her: she seemed even smaller than she had when he had first seen her from up here, and further away, although she hadn't moved. He couldn't find words to answer her. He looked back at the line and scanned it for a truck, but the only vehicles he saw were overloaded carts pulled along by their owners. Further away, to the east of Pillau, the River Pregel flowed into the bay beneath the ice. Another line was stretched across the frozen water: more civilians attempting to flee.

As he squinted into the distance, he heard the drone of an aeroplane and searched the horizon. At first he couldn't see anything, but then towards Königsberg he spotted a plane flying straight for him, with another behind it, and a third. His mother shouted to him from below, but he could not hear what she had said above the noise of the engines. As they approached, they broke their formation. The first plane banked south towards the people on the ice, while the other two continued to fly west. Then the second plane peeled off to line itself up with the road to Fischhausen. His mother was still screaming up to him, but Peter was too mesmerised by the planes to turn away. The one over the ice began to descend. Then the third plane was approaching him, high overhead. As it flew over, he heard a burst of staccato machine-gun fire. On the frozen bay the line scattered, as the first plane's machine-guns strafed the ice. Then the line closer to him fragmented. People fled in every direction, leaving their carts and bags in the middle of the road as the second plane strafed it, then veered away to rejoin its original flight path over the Baltic to the west.

Peter was transfixed by the chaos unfolding below him. Later, he would learn that he had observed the first stage of one of the largest ethnic flights in history, which began as millions fled their ancestral homes to escape the advancing Russian front and continued after the war's conclusion through forced expulsion, displacing twelve to fourteen million Central and Eastern European ethnic Germans, civilian refugees, of whom more than a million would perish before they reached the west.

BOOK IV

Journey to the Empire's Centre

Chapter 1

Peter slid back through the small opening into the water tower and was climbing down the rungs when Ida stuck her head through the doorway and peered up to him. 'Are you there?' she called.

'I'm on my way down.'

When he reached the ground, she was waiting for him. 'There's a line of people,' he said. 'Hundreds . . . thousands.'

'Thousands?' Ida asked. Evidently she thought he was exaggerating. Peter didn't answer her.

Ida and the children went back to the road. Within a few minutes they were rounding a bend and walked straight into a crowd. Ida slowed and turned to Peter. 'Are there more?'

Close by, an old man was struggling to stand, with a pool of blood at his feet. He was holding his stomach as if he felt ill. But when Peter looked at him carefully he saw that the man was holding his intestines, to stop them spilling on to the ground. An elderly woman was trying to press them back into the hole from which his ruptured viscera protruded.

Sickened, Peter turned away, then glanced skywards.

No one seemed to know what to do. Ida had gone to the man to help, but he shrieked out at everyone to keep away from him. Peter looked at Otto. They knew the man was dying. Peter grabbed his mother's arm. 'Let's go.'

When they reached the main road, Ida looked out for faces she knew. Surely she would recognise someone, but she saw only strangers. Before they joined the column she said to the children, 'Hold hands. We mustn't lose each other now.'

She checked to make sure that they had firm hold of each other, then guided them into the flow to merge with the river of refugees. When they had settled in its rhythm, they glanced around. Suitcases, clothing, books, kitchenware and pictures in broken frames lay scattered everywhere across the icy ground, with the occasional old man or woman. Every so often they passed a mother weeping over an infant, its face tinted blue like the ice. Many refugees appeared to be sleepwalking, while others weren't walking at all: dead from disease, hypothermia or starvation.

Ida tried to keep the children from paying attention to the roadside. But the more she reprimanded them, the more curious they became. She finally ignored the roadside herself, content with her children's close and constant contact with her. As they neared Pillau the pace slowed, so Ida, who knew her way around the town, led the children away from the column, weaving through backstreets and alleys, which were filled with almost as many refugees as the main avenue.

When they reached the local Hitler Youth headquarters, she turned right into a narrow alley that ended at the water's edge. Pillau was on a tiny peninsula that hung like an elephant's trunk off the south-west end from the main Samland peninsula, creating a natural bay to its east. They gazed across the water and saw boats and ships tied up to the sea wall, while more waited in the bay.

The family went from vessel to vessel, trying to find a boat on which to secure passage, but at each one they were turned away. Every gangplank was crammed with people pushing aboard. Ida overheard a woman say that Hitler had agreed three days ago to allow refugees to evacuate to the west.

When they reached the lighthouse at the tip of the Pillau peninsula, they stood patiently at the end of a long line that split into five fingers as it neared the docks, where boats were taking aboard as many people as they could manage without sinking. For the first thirty minutes after they arrived the queue inched forward, then stopped and eventually inched forward again. After an hour they were directed to a line leading off to the right. The large fishing boat on which they hoped to find places had been filled by the time they were nearing the gangplank. People were pressed tightly together on the deck and even the roof of the captain's quarters was packed with people holding on to each other so that they wouldn't fall into the bay. A crewman came down the plank and stood behind Ida. 'Everyone from here forward,' he said to her.

'But my children are behind you.'

The crewman pushed them forward.

Someone behind them swore at him.

'Any more of that and you won't be going anywhere,' he roared.

'We can't wait all night.'

'Better that than the rest of your life.'

The sailor pushed Ida and the children in front of him until they were on the ship. They squeezed between passengers, following him now, until they reached a doorway. He shoved a woman aside and led them down a steep flight of stairs towards the last remaining space, the engine vibrating against their feet. At the bottom of the stairs he pushed aside more people, and yelled to Ida and the children, 'Hurry!' When they reached another door the sailor forced more people out of the way. He pulled open a steel door and petrol fumes billowed out. The noise of the engine was deafening now. The sailor beckoned and Ida pulled the children into the room. As they went in, other passengers shouted at them and tried to push them back out.

'Careful!' the sailor yelled. 'Keep away from the engine!' It was emitting a dense, almost liquid heat that was nearly unbearable after the brittle cold outside.

They slid along the wall until they reached the back, where an elderly man was clinging to a narrow lip. Above the engine noise they heard the door clang shut.

Ida was developing a headache from the fumes when the engine, less than a metre from her, revved. The boat was preparing to leave port.

'You're lucky,' the old man beside Peter shouted.

'What?'

'I said you're lucky,' the man bellowed into Peter's ear, 'to get a place down here.'

The engine continued to rev and a woman collapsed in a corner. A group of teenage boys kicked open the door to let in some fresher air.

When the commotion had subsided Peter turned back to the old man. 'Why are we lucky?'

'If we're hit by a torpedo, we'll die straight away.' The man grinned. 'We won't have to swim around waiting to drown like everyone on deck.'

Peter supposed he was right. After all, the man was as old as his grandfather and must know about war. Peter decided not to think any more about his stroke of good fortune and instead occupied his thoughts with the secret tunnel that afforded an escape route for the monks of Germau. He squinted, until he could see only the outline of the people lining the walls opposite, illuminated by the single bulb a few feet above him. He pretended he was in the tunnel, surrounded by villagers waiting in candlelight for their leader's orders. Perhaps there were two passageways, Peter thought.

The overloaded vessel pulled away from the sea wall and moved out into the harbour, filled with boats and vast chunks of floating ice – an ice-breaker was going back and forth across the bay, keeping clear both ships at anchor and the channel to the sea. Rough seas waited and when the boat reached open water it bobbed and heaved in the heavy swell. The refugees on deck scrambled for handholds, grabbing the stanchion bars and each other to stop themselves slipping into the icy water. In the engine room the refugees clung to the beams that reinforced the steel walls to keep themselves away from the burning engine.

The dull pounding of the pistons in their thick steel sleeves carried up from the engine room, like a damaged church bell calling the faithful to prayer. The boat had to travel only a short distance out into the Baltic before heading south-east to Danzig, but everyone knew that although the voyage would be relatively short it was still long enough for catastrophe to strike. It had been only a little over a week since the *Gustloff* was sunk.

As soon as the Pillau lighthouse disappeared from view, the captain zigzagged through the water, like a yacht tacking into a headwind, attempting to confuse and elude the Russian submarines that lurked below. The manoeuvre would double the distance to their destination and the refugees were flung from port to starboard and back, as the vessel changed course without warning at sharp angles. Leyna was sick. Peter vomited over the feet of the old man beside him.

Some time later the boat stopped and bobbed in the sea,

while the crew turned on small engines up on deck to create a thick cloud of steam to camouflage it. The captain had had a radio message: planes were heading in their direction. As the fog machines churned to life, engulfing them in a mist so that the ship appeared from above to be little more than a wisp of fog gathering at sea, some of those on deck, who had nodded off with exhaustion, woke up and thought they must be in heaven.

Chapter 2

When the boat docked at Danzig, those on deck and in the corridors disembarked first. As Ida and the children waited their turn to get off, she realised from the way that the boys were shouting at her that they were having difficulty in hearing, although the engine had been shut down. On dock, the fresh air restored them, but after the rolling of the ship they had lost their balance on land. Ida staggered to a bench and collapsed on to it to wait for her equilibrium to return. Leyna sat beside her, holding her arm, while the boys continued to test their legs.

Eventually, they held hands and moved into the city's streets. They followed a throng to the railway station but before they got to it a man told Ida that cattle trucks were being loaded with people near the edge of the city. They heard rumours from other refugees that the waiting trucks would depart for Berlin that evening when a locomotive arrived. Someone said they should return to the harbour to take a ship for Denmark and another insisted that the only way to Berlin was on foot. An old woman had told Ida that there was no way out of Danzig – that the Russians would arrive at any minute. It seemed that everyone they spoke to had heard a different rumour.

The one they heard most often, though, was the one Ida

155

most wanted to hear: that cattle trucks were waiting at the edge of the city to take them west. She knew that boats were sailing for Denmark, but she didn't want to go there: she wanted to get to Berlin, where Elsa would take them in. She had heard that boats were stopping at Stettin, the Baltic port north of Berlin, but decided to go by train, even if it took longer. She had had enough of the sea after one voyage. She chose to ignore a rumour that the cattle trucks had been standing in sidings for more than a week, crammed with frightened refugees.

Exhausted, hungry and cold, the family moved on. The cool logic that had sustained Ida through the flight across the peninsula had left her now that she was in a strange, war-torn city. No one knew where they were supposed to go and everyone seemed disorientated in the maze of Danzig's streets.

Ida and the children rounded a corner and collided with a group racing in the opposite direction. They regained their footing, and Ida asked where the others thought the train might be. As they talked a second group ran past. Without another word, they all turned and followed.

Eventually they came to a set of tracks where a long line of cattle trucks was parked beneath a row of trees, with a crowd gathering beside them. Some were trying to squeeze inside as others climbed on to the roofs. Ida picked up Leyna and ran with the boys to the last truck. It was already packed with people and suitcases. Stacks of abandoned luggage lay on the ground.

Ida lifted in the children one at a time, then climbed up behind them, ignoring the passengers' protests, and forced her way into the crowded interior. She thought, briefly, of Karl, wondering if he was anywhere near Danzig. The truck was so tightly packed that everyone had to stand upright. The parents of younger children checked constantly that the little ones were not being trampled or squeezed too tightly to breathe. But at least they were warm – there was no room for even a draught to penetrate between the wedged bodies.

The trucks stood where they were for the rest of the afternoon and, as darkness fell, there was silence outside. No clanking metal as a locomotive was hooked to the cattle trucks and no roar of an engine down the line. No one got out for fear of losing his or her place and containers were passed round for people to urinate.

Before sunrise the metal walls began to vibrate, shaking the occupants out of half-consciousness. Then the truck jerked and there were screams as some were crushed under the weight of others thrown against them. When they had all regained their balance, they felt the throb of an engine vibrate through the truck.

Half an hour later, word came that the train would depart that evening, in twelve hours' time. The engineer couldn't risk a daylight run because there were frequent aerial raids. A handful of boys jumped out to scavenge for food for their families.

After dusk the locomotive sprang to life, a low hum sounding through the trucks. An hour later it lurched forward and the trucks rumbled down the tracks. An eruption of voices filled the interior, elated to be moving at last, but many were despondent too: they were leaving the only corner of the world they had ever known.

The journey from Danzig to Berlin normally took a little over a day, but by dawn they had barely reached the next town, where they stopped beneath another stretch of trees. Those who had been unable to find room inside and had clung to the tops of the trucks back in Danzig to avoid missing their only ride west now climbed down, frostbitten, and joined the long lines of refugees walking west along rural roads. In the trucks the children who were small enough to squeeze to the floor between the adults took turns to kneel and rub their parents' and grandparents' legs to keep the blood flowing – most were unable to stretch or sit. At dusk, the train moved off again. Some passengers were curled up in corners, shivering or, alternatively, showing no sign of life at all. Most still huddled together, listening to the person breathing beside them, life encouraging life. When they stopped again on the third day, the train had covered less ground than it had the previous night, stopping at one point for more than three hours on a side track to let a military train through to the east.

Ida realised the journey might take as long as a week and decided to risk getting out to find food for the children. Leyna had been crying with hunger. It was on the outskirts of the town that Ida spotted a chicken coop. There had been no food in the shops they had passed and she was desperate now. She, Otto and Leyna hid in some bushes while Peter slipped in and took a few freshly laid eggs, then sprinted to his family as the farmer came out to investigate his hens' squawks of alarm. Carefully Ida punctured a hole in the top of each shell, then she and the children took turns to suck the contents.

That night, on the move again, the woman beside Ida was holding a baby whose little face had turned grey. At first everyone ignored them – they understood how she felt: she wanted to keep it with her until she could bury it near where she settled. Most knew, too, that a few mothers were carrying their own dead infants in their luggage to bury them in the west. Eventually another woman persuaded the young mother to let her and some others bury the baby when the train stopped for the day. They would make a proper marker for the grave, she said, and the woman agreed.

At night, they stood in the dark listening to the air howling beneath the train, the rattling and clanking of the steel wheels rolling along the metal tracks. No one spoke – eveyone was conserving what remained of their energy and hope.

On the fifth day more people ventured off the train to scour the villages for any scraps of food and water. At last they had left the front: the enemy and the fighting were behind them for now. Bombers still passed overhead, but they reserved their payload for urban targets further east. The Polish plains beyond the villages seemed to go on for ever. At the horizon the earth fell away with no view of the next town or even distant trees. The emptiness unsettled the refugees, whose spirits were raised by a lone telephone pole alongside a stretch of bombed roadway, a distant grove of trees or even a cloud. Now everything, living or not, was invested with a significance it had never had in East Prussia. A discarded milk can was a promise of food to come and spent shell casings a reminder of the war they had left behind and the peace that awaited them in the west.

The only constant across the landscape, day after day, was the endless column of refugees, clogging the roads of the towns and villages at which the train stopped each morning, people who had not found room on the train or had decided that they would be better off journeying by land.

Chapter 3

To fend off boredom during the periods they spent waiting –
delays that sometimes stretched to two or three days when military trains had to be allowed through at night – Peter and Otto
collected bomb fragments, planning to sell the scrap metal in
Berlin and buy food with the money. But when they showed
their treasure to Ida she snapped, 'Take that rubbish away!'

'But we can sell it!' Peter protested.

'It's true,' Otto added. 'I've been to salvage yards with my
father.'

'I doubt if it's worth much now. Go and find something
useful to do.'

'We'll hide it, then come back after the war and collect it.'

Each morning Ida sent the boys out to find food – she had
learned that children were treated more sympathetically than
adult scavengers. When they came back, she shared out whatever they had found between them all, then slept for the rest
of the day. At night they had to be ready for the train's departure and when it did move it was almost impossible to sleep,
with many people falling on to others. There was comfort in
having another body pressed close, but usually they pretended
not to notice each other.

Although they were hungry all the time, the boys had more

energy than Leyna or Ida. Sometimes, when they were foraging, refugees passing through the villages mistook them for members of their own procession and gave them crusts or a small quantity of lard from a jar hidden in a coat pocket.

Many refugees failed to find enough to sustain themselves on the journey. Later, Otto discovered that his paternal grandmother had left her village near the Ukrainian border to join the migration west. He never heard from or saw her again. Other villagers had seen her join the line but had lost track of her when they became preoccupied with their own survival. Sometimes they paused to bury the dead, hoping others would do the same for them, but the weak often left the line to find their own spot to rest for ever. This proved the most dignified exit for elders not wanting to bring attention to their suffering.

The truth was that few wanted to hear about anyone else's problems. If a man was with his wife or daughter who had been raped, the woman often felt worse for her husband's or father's suffering than she did about her own: he carried the shame of having been unable to defend her. Those men rarely spoke. The violated women were usually silent too, but those who were not risked the disapproval of others, who considered they brought even more shame to their *Familie* by drawing attention to what had befallen them.

Sometimes an older woman would growl, 'Hold your tongue, whore. Be happy you're not dead.' These self-appointed matriarchs – seemingly bitter but often only bent on the survival of their clan – proved the most effective means of self-censorship. Ironically, they were the women who gave food to Peter and Otto. They usually walked alone, like a shepherd tending a flock, watching from a distance to see that everyone kept together. The lines of refugees appeared continuous, but at close quarters an insider would sense family, clan and village units.

While these women could be severe, there was tenderness in them too, which only emerged when those in need did not appeal directly for help. If the boys asked outright for food, they were rewarded with a lash from a switch beneath the woman's coat, which snapped through the air so quickly that they never saw it coming. Once, after being whipped and fleeing a matriarch's wrath, the boys were stopped less than a kilometre down the line by a woman from a different village who had mistaken the pain in their face from their recent beating for the silent suffering of hunger and smeared a spot of lard on their palms from her secret reserve without saying a word or letting them thank her.

Chapter 4

The following week the train reached the outskirts of Berlin, where Otto took over as leader – Ida and Peter had never been there. He didn't know the part of the city where the train had stopped, but he had a strong sense of direction, which Ida thought had sharpened now that he would soon see his mother, as long as he could get them to the centre.

Berlin was nothing like she had envisaged it, Ida thought. She had imagined it would be similar to Königsberg, but its sheer size intimidated her. She looked around her in trepidation as Otto led them on. The destruction was far worse than she had expected. The idea of travelling west to find safety now seemed ludicrous. The area they entered had been razed to the ground. She realised it would be her fault if anything happened now to the children. She had had no option, however, but to flee.

Otto darted ahead to ask directions and Ida was almost overcome with the emotions she had suppressed since they fled Germau. So that she didn't break down in front of the children, she pretended they had arrived in Königsberg and were heading for her parents' apartment, that her mother was still alive. It was nearly Christmas, she imagined, and the children would sing carols with their grandparents. When she returned to Germau, Paul would be waiting for them, working overtime as always to make sure everyone had festive goose . . .

After they had been walking for a couple of hours, often scrambling over rubble, the river came into view. It made Ida understand that her journey, in which she had been guided only by the instinct to keep the children alive, was ending – yet she was filled with sadness. She followed Otto towards the embankment, holding herself in check, but she knew she would soon give way to tears. She fell back as Otto pressed on, eager to be home.

Peter called to his cousin to wait, then turned back to his mother. 'What's wrong?'

That was all it took. She stopped and buried her face in her hands, but instead of tears, as she had expected, she began to giggle. The children ran up to her, confused. She lowered her hands and tried to control herself, but could only laugh harder. Seconds later, without anyone knowing why, they were all laughing. Tears streamed down Ida's face; the children slumped to the ground, holding their stomachs as they laughed uncontrollably. With tears flowing freely from their eyes, Ida reached out and pulled the children closer.

Chapter 5

'Are you sure you know where you're going, Otto?' Ida asked, when they started off again.

'It's up here,' he assured her.

Although Berlin had little of Königsberg's charm – there was no ancient castle in the centre, no island with a cathedral in the river – there were lindens growing in perfect rows. They had reached Unter den Linden, which reminded her of East Prussia, with its ranks of trees, like the country roads at home, from which, perhaps, the city planners had taken the idea to decorate the boulevard. After all, she thought, Königsberg was the historic heart of Prussia. She remembered her old schoolmaster who had taught her that it had become the first Protestant state when the bishop of Samland embraced Luther's teachings at Christmas mass in 1523.

'Look!' Otto exclaimed. 'The Brandenburg Gate.'

He sounded as though he had met an old friend, she thought, and perhaps in a way he had. Less than a block from the gate, Otto stopped and said they must turn back – he had missed the street. He ran back to Wilhelmstrasse. Then he beckoned them to follow him. They had walked a few hundred metres down the side street when a guard stopped them. Ahead Ida saw a large, familiar-looking building through the trees – the

Chancellery, she realised with a shock. The guard would not let them pass.

'But my mother and father, they work there.' Otto began to cry.

'We've come all the way from East Prussia,' Ida told the sentry. 'My sister, Elsa, is a secretary.'

'Orders. No one passes, not even sisters.'

Ida wasn't amused. She tried, but failed to persuade him to deliver a message to see if she was there, then told the children to go back to the boulevard. There, Otto strode ahead. 'Are you sure you know where you're going?' Ida called.

'Yes.'

He had led them to the Chancellery, hoping to surprise his mother, Ida thought. Soon he had turned into another side street and was taking them past a series of bombed buildings. Young children were playing among the rubble, while older children and their mothers moved stones from the pavement in a futile effort to tidy their surroundings. No one greeted the family as they passed.

Eventually Otto stopped at a junction, turned left and pointed to a cul-de-sac, flanked on three sides by enormous apartment buildings. Each had been bombed and those on the right and left had caved in completely; only the one directly in front still had its basic shape. She asked Otto what he was pointing at. 'My parents' apartment.'

Ida studied Otto's face. He appeared untroubled by the destruction that confronted them. He looked up at his aunt and cousins. 'What are we waiting for?' his expression seemed to ask.

Peter and Leyna ran after him. Ida saw that the ruins were simply part of the world in which they were growing up, neither bad nor good, just there. She shivered at the idea. They hadn't expected Berlin to be any different. Even Otto, who had lived most of his life in the city, didn't seem surprised by the destruction surrounding him, as though he had already accepted that his home might have gone. Perhaps, Ida thought, he had taken them to the Chancellery first because he had expected it after what he had seen since they had got off the train.

The top corners of Otto's building had crumbled inwards and the roofs of the apartments on the outside edge of the building had caved in. Every window had been blown out. Otto pointed now towards a window on the second floor near the middle of the building.

The stairs were covered with rubble and dust, but someone had cleared a path up. Otto went up to the first landing, then on to the second. Ida paused, before hurrying after him – she had to be with him in case he found something that upset him. They came to a darkened hallway, where shafts of broken light entered through large cracks in the walls, and peered through a door frame – the door itself had gone.

A woman was sitting with her daughter and an infant. They stared at Ida and Otto without speaking.

The family turned away and Otto ran on up the hall towards his apartment. When they reached it, the door had been propped up on its frame. Otto began to slide it to the side. Ida stopped him and knocked. No one answered, so Otto continued to move the door until he heard a sound inside. 'Mutti,' he called.

Ida heard hushed voices, none of which sounded like her sister. She knocked again but still there was no reply. She went into a large, empty room. Her eyes fell on a heap of pans stacked neatly on the kitchen floor, near a makeshift fireplace constructed from rubble.

In the living room she found an old man and woman sitting on the floor.

'Do you live here?' Ida asked.

'What does it look like?' the man replied.

From his accent, Ida and Otto knew he wasn't a Berliner.

'Where are you from?'

From Ida's accent they realised she wasn't a Berliner, either.

'Silesia,' the man answered. 'Breslau.'

'We're from East Prussia,' Ida told him. 'My sister, Elsa, lives here. This is her boy,' she said.

The couple glanced at him and smiled. 'Otto?' the man asked.

The fact that a stranger knew Otto's name . . . Ida broke down. This time she neither laughed nor cried, but the man could tell something was wrong. He hauled himself to his feet and embraced her. 'Elsa is safe. She's at work but she'll be home before dark. She's told us all about you and Otto. She has been kind enough to let us stay here with her.'

Chapter 6

'He's gone to Russia,' Elsa said, answering Ida's question about her husband Konrad. 'Where is Karl?'

'I don't know,' Ida said.

'He hasn't written?'

'We haven't been home. He left a few weeks before us.' Then, to change the subject, Ida asked, 'Do you still work at the Chancellery? We went there.'

'Not any more.' She had been let go but had since found a job as a housekeeper, although she didn't know how long it would last either since her employers wanted to leave Berlin. 'They have several maids. I'm worried. It's hard to find work.'

Each night the sisters lay awake whispering. The children slept close to them for warmth as the bitter winter wind blew through the broken windows. The old Silesian had tried to stop the draught with planks. Elsa had invited the couple to stay with her when she had found them wandering around the city one evening on her way home from work. Her building had been hit just three days before. Most of her neighbours who had survived the raid had since abandoned the city for smaller towns, their apartments uninhabitable. Elsa had been frightened alone in the building and the elderly couple had made her feel safer, she said.

Shortly after their reunion, however, the sisters began to resent the Silesians since they lacked the energy or endurance to go about the city looking for food each day, yet still consumed their share. Ida and the children settled into a routine, rising early to go out to collect food and wood scraps for the fire. To relieve their resentment, the sisters assigned the Silesians to forage in a nearby neighbourhood, where they often had more success. This way, if they did find something to eat, they could share it as the sisters did with the food they collected elsewhere.

Besides collecting food and fuel, cooking and cleaning, the main activity the two families shared each evening was exchanging rumours they heard about East Prussia or Silesia, Königsberg or Breslau. Everywhere they went they bumped into refugees. They would first ask about their homes, then about other areas. They would also reel off the names of their relatives, followed by those of their apartment mates. Many refugees were reunited through word of mouth. While refugees shared stories about relatives finding each other, Ida's only chance encounter happened one afternoon when she bumped into her father-in-law's cousin Ulf near Alexanderplatz. He appeared worried as if he were being followed. She asked if he had heard anything about Paul or Karl.

'No, nothing.' He lowered his head and prayed with her, then shoved a small amount of money into her hand before disappearing into the crowd without saying goodbye.

Chapter 7

The security that Ida had expected to find in the capital had proved illusory. For now she didn't fear an imminent invasion by the Russians as much as she dreaded the air raids that struck like clockwork every second day. She also learned that most locals didn't like the refugees. One woman she had begged food from had gone so far as to blame Ida and the other eastern Germans for the war. Ida had found her accusation absurd, but soon realised that many Berliners felt the same in their own private attempts to protect themselves from a war that had come home.

'That's not true,' Elsa said. 'Berliners have always welcomed outsiders.' She told Ida she was overreacting.

Ida left the subject alone. After all, the boys were happy in Berlin.

Each afternoon they played in the rubble, searching for more metal and other buried treasure. They still had plans to make a fortune from the scraps when the war ended. One afternoon they ran home screaming that they were going to be millionaires.

When the sisters asked them why they were so excited, they grabbed their mothers' wrists and pulled them across the yard.

'The Führer will make us heroes!' Peter said.

The women followed them through the neighbourhood, climbing over a pile of broken bricks as though they were little girls themselves. The boys had carefully covered their treasure with a piece of cloth so nobody else would claim it. Otto gently peeled it back to show their mothers an unexploded bomb. 'It'll save us from the Russians. A miracle bomb,' he said, repeating a rumour he had heard about a bomb that would help Germany win the war.

The sisters were horrified, too scared to scream, petrified that if the boys dropped the cloth too fast it might explode.

At their parents' shock, the boys became scared themselves. They dropped the cloth and ran over to them. Peter felt his mother's arms trembling. The four stood motionless at the bottom of the brick pile, frightened that if they climbed out, a brick might fall on the bomb and detonate it. Elsa looked around to find the safest way out without disrupting any loose bricks. She decided to climb out the same way they had come in, hoping all the bricks had settled in that area. Although only three metres up one side and down the other, it felt like the longest six metres they had ever crossed. The sisters waited until they were down the block, then turned and whipped the boys with a switch.

A few days later the government announced a programme to relocate refugees within Germany. Berliners, however, weren't eligible, which meant that Elsa and Otto had to stay in the city. The family made plans to register together anyway. They decided to say they were all refugees, which in a sense was true since Elsa had an East Prussian birth certificate. In fact, only Otto had been born in Berlin – they would pretend his papers had been lost during the exodus.

Even without papers, the officer had merely glanced at them, taking brief notice of Ida's dark hair, her nose and eyes, before filling out a form declaring them East Prussian and thus eligible. They were listed as one family. The officer asked Ida's surname – when he couldn't spell it, he asked her to write it.

'German?' he asked.

Ida became nervous, but before she could say anything, he said all kinds of strange names showed up at the office every day now, that nobody would ever guess were German. She recalled her father-in-law's reply years ago to Hitler's statement that Baltic Germans 'seemed to possess some negative sort of quality and at the very same time to assume an air of superiority, of being masters of everything. I often find it difficult to get on with them.'

'He finds it difficult,' Ferdinand had told her, 'because we're not quite as pure as he wishes we were.' Her husband's side took great, albeit silent, pride that despite the centuries they had never Germanised their Balt-Prussian surname.

To ensure there were no more questions, the sisters pestered the man about their husbands off fighting on the Eastern Front: 'How can we find out where they are? We haven't heard from them in months!'

He became irritated at their enquiry, worried they might burst into tears. He thrust their documents into Ida's hands, then directed them to another office to find out about their husbands. 'Check the lists out front every day to see if we've found sponsors for you,' he finished. 'Be ready to leave when you see your name.'

BOOK V

Towards the New World

Chapter 1

Although minor tensions remained, they continued to share their living quarters with the Silesian family, who had also registered for relocation. They wanted to leave Berlin now that the opportunity had presented itself, but Elsa worried that they might sabotage her own plans by reporting that she wasn't a refugee, merely a Berliner posing as one, so that they could get her and Otto's spots on the train.

'Don't worry,' Ida said. 'You took them in. I don't think they'll pay you back by ruining your chances.' But Ida did agree that people were becoming more remote from each other in the city as more bombs fell, more refugees arrived and food grew scarce.

Even in its ruined condition – bitter air blowing through shattered windows – they still felt fortunate to live in the building, away from the riff-raff wandering the streets below at night. Parts of the city were still in good shape, such as a section near Schöneberg where Ida often walked. She had found a baker there who sometimes gave the children crusts, while she hid round the corner. She liked the Tiergarten too, at least the trees, but there were too many refugees living there now, desperate for food and shelter, for her to feel safe.

Wandering around one afternoon three weeks later, she saw her name on the board at the relocation office. It was closed

177

that afternoon, so she and Elsa woke early the next morning and went there before it opened. A long line had gathered. When it was finally their turn at noon, they were told to get ready to depart that night. They raced home to grab their suitcase, which they had already packed.

The Silesians shared their excitement since it could only mean, they assumed, that they would soon leave the city too. Nonetheless, the sisters were nervous that something might go wrong. Elsa was unfamiliar with the station on the edge of the city where they were told to go. When they set off, though, they soon met other refugees on their way there and found out that it wasn't a station at all – just a place along the tracks where the train had been concealed under trees.

Once on the train, they sat patiently waiting for nightfall. When it got dark they sat without speaking, worried they might be stuck there for days. But less than two hours later the engine came to life, its familiar vibration humming through the train. It idled another hour, inspectors running up and down the tracks, more families arriving. People outside shouted as others stood together crying.

When the train did move, it crawled at such a slow pace that Ida felt she could walk faster. She knew the reason for travelling under the veil of darkness but no one mentioned it: to hide from the bombers hidden in the night sky searching for targets below, especially convoys and trains. Unable to travel under the full moon, their lives were partially restricted by the alignment of the stars. The train picked up speed and moved into the countryside, swaying back and forth as though the engineer might lose control at a sharp bend. Air howled and pressed through the windows.

The sisters, unable to see each other in the dark, held hands under the blanket. Neither was overtly religious, but both focused so intently on their separate prayers that they didn't notice they were slowing down less than two hours later. The stop proved disappointing. No one got off. Voices moved along the train and a door on the truck behind them clicked open, then clanged shut. There followed a long silence, before they started forward again, hurtling through the night.

Ida's mind wandered back to the plains of East Prussia – scattered bogs, swamps and lakes carved into the surface by receding glaciers. Her thoughts moved back in time through the darkness: the vast pine forests covering Samland slowly sinking beneath the rising sea, sinking even as the trees grew until only the tops protruded above the churning waters, before being buried not only underneath water but under the earth itself . . . until an epochal shift between tides forced the sea to retreat again from the land, the ancient forests creeping back to the surface, revealing fragments of golden, gemlike shards along the coast – until soon cultures from afar were trading the petrified blood from the rising graveyards of dead trees into the make-up and design of their own artefacts, the sap of ancient pines disseminating themselves across the earth – a living body, a consciousness, a being . . .

Ida felt someone shaking her awake.

'We're here,' Elsa said.

Ida rubbed her eyes and sat up. It was still dark outside. The man who had checked her papers when boarding called her name. She heard the children rustle at her side. 'Get ready,' she said.

When she stepped off the train, she saw a row of worn buildings beside the tracks and nothing more. She wondered if they were dropping them off in the middle of nowhere to get rid of them. In the faint light she could see gentle hills rising into mountains behind the buildings. She turned to the man shouting at the other families to descend.

'Thuringia,' he said, anticipating her question.

'Thuringia,' Ida muttered to herself. She had heard the name before, knew Bach was born somewhere nearby, that Goethe and Schiller had lived in Weimar – the image of Schiller's statue on the square near her parents' Königsberg apartment flashed into her mind. She had always loved geology and history – it let her escape the present – but soon the statue faded, replaced by a horse-drawn wagon parked next to one of the buildings. A farmer patiently waited for everyone to get off the train. *We're so far from home*, she thought; and then, *Will we ever go back? Stop it*, she told herself. *We're safe.*

Chapter 2

After the train left they waited in the dark, unsure what to do next.

The farmer approached with a scrap of paper on which he had scribbled a name. 'Ida?' he enquired.

The other families asked where they were supposed to go and he assured them that more people were coming to get them. Then he told the sisters and their children to come with him. He introduced himself as Gerhard, picked up their only suitcase and put it in the carriage. He helped the women on to the wagon, lifted each child, setting the boys in the back and the little girl with the sisters up front.

Sensing it more awkward to stay silent than to make light of the circumstances that had brought them together, he joked, 'Light travellers.' Then he glanced to make sure he hadn't missed anything.

'Never cared for baggage,' Elsa said, not missing a beat.

Gerhard grinned.

'To be honest, we were expecting a motorcar with a chauffeur. What's a woman to do these days?' Elsa added.

This time he laughed, lifted the reins and slapped the horses, who began moving through Uhlstädt. They soon reached a narrow dirt road that climbed for two kilometres through the trees. It had been difficult to see in the dark before entering the forest, but now it was impossible as they started the climb.

'How do the horses stay on the road?' Elsa asked.

'They guide me,' he assured her. 'They'll stop if they can't find their way. It doesn't matter if I want them to continue. Owning horses is a bit like the old saying about a house – you don't own it, it owns you.'

The sisters had never heard the saying before. They giggled at the thought of the horses owning Gerhard.

When they reached the treeline, dawn illuminated the sky enough to see the silhouette of the chapel and its miniature bell tower.

'Partschefeld,' Gerhard said. 'Home.'

As they neared a tree in the middle of a small junction that marked the centre of the village, Gerhard stopped the wagon and helped Ida down. He walked her and her children to the closest house. A woman opened the door before Gerhard had even knocked. She introduced herself as Jutta Joachim.

'Frau Joachim?' Ida repeated.

'Yes, yes,' she replied.

A wave of sadness swept through Ida. She bowed her head. The unexpected mention of her brother's name, in her weary state, rang out like an incantation calling him back from the dead. He had drowned one morning when she was a child, after they had run down to the lake. He had swum out too far. The wind picked up. She watched helplessly from the shallows, too young to assist and unsure whether he was playing a game. By the time her father had heard Ida screaming it was too late. Joachim was gone. Although only six at the time, she had since carried the guilt of his death. In as few words as possible, Ida told Frau Joachim that her late brother had the same name.

Frau Joachim apologised and said it was fine for her and the children to call her Jutta.

'No,' Ida said. She felt embarrassed. She had not meant to present herself full of self-pity and sadness, but neither had she expected to hear Joachim's name. She had forgotten his given name served as a surname in other parts of Germany. *God prepares*, she said to herself in silent prayer, murmuring the meaning of her dead brother's name, that of the father of the Virgin Mary.

Frau Joachim waved the children into the house, then took hold of Ida's hand and led her inside. Gerhard returned to his wagon and took Elsa and Otto up to his house, where they would live with him and his wife.

The smell of meat cooking in the closed house was so overwhelming that Ida had to sit down. She had not been in a well-insulated house for months, much less one rich with scents of warm food. Frau Joachim said she had woken early that morning to prepare breakfast for them. The children were impatient at the smell of food, but followed their mother's example and stood quietly near her chair.

Frau Joachim insisted a second time that the children call her Jutta. She preferred to be informal in her own home. She was a widow, had given birth to a single child – a boy, grown, gone and killed earlier in the war in Hungary. She told Ida it was an honour to be hostess to her and the children. 'It gets lonely,' she said.

Ida smiled and offered to help in the kitchen.

'No need.' Jutta showed her the bedroom instead. She knew she was tired from the journey. She could see that the children needed to eat as she straightened the bed for Ida to lie down. 'They can help me while you rest a little.'

Ida agreed without speaking, her body language indicating approval. Even though she hadn't eaten a full meal since leaving

Germau, the food's overwhelming smell hurt her stomach. She leaned back on the bed and lay down, sinking deep into the feather mattress, the first soft bed she had lain on in months. She thought about Karl. Where had they taken him? Then Paul: she was still angry, an emotion she used to cover the hurt that he had not the common decency to write to her in Germau, when the woman in the neighbouring village had received a letter each month from her husband in the same division. She reprimanded herself for having such thoughts and returned to the one that most grounded her: at least she was safe – for it was safety, she knew, that provided the luxury to ponder resentment.

She heard Leyna giggling. She tried to recall the last time she had heard her laugh. Their hysterics in Berlin, she knew, had not been joy, no matter how hard they had laughed. She sank deeper into the mattress, her eyes heavy. She forced them open to stay awake for breakfast. She breathed as deeply as possible, held in the air, then exhaled, focusing on the air leaving her lungs. She inhaled again, this time more slowly, and held it longer, then let it escape as she started to feel more in tune with her body. She felt a needle of pain and reached down between her legs. When she touched herself it seemed to disappear. She noticed a mild discomfort in her lower abdomen. Hunger? Her eyes began to close again and this time she didn't try to keep them open.

Chapter 3

When Ida woke twenty-four hours later, her sister was standing at her bedside with the children and Jutta. 'She'll be fine. It's been a long journey.'

'I was concerned is all,' Jutta said.

'Is breakfast ready?' Ida asked, unaware that it was the morning following her arrival.

'Warm and waiting,' Jutta said. 'Whenever you wish.'

That afternoon, after Ida had slowly eaten her first full meal in months, the sisters walked with the children along the farm track cutting through the fields in which the villagers were working. Gerhard came over to say hello, glancing cautiously at Elsa.

'It's nothing,' Elsa said.

'I hope not, because your vacation ends tomorrow,' he joked. Then he turned to the children. 'I hope you like dirt. It's hard work preparing the soil. We need all the hands we can get.'

'We'll be ready. It's nice to be needed for a change,' Ida said.

After leaving Gerhard they strolled towards the forest. At the top of a hill they turned back and looked at the village below. Otto counted thirty-one houses. A flock of geese ran across the yard of a farmhouse bordering the fields.

They soon settled into the villagers' routine, rising early each morning, eating breakfast, then helping with whatever tasks their sponsors needed done. Almost everything revolved around keeping food on the table, except on Sundays when they attended chapel at the one-room structure. The travelling pastor often prayed for abundant harvests and good weather. Most tasks were done by hand, but there were seven horses in the village for ploughing and hauling.

At first Jutta had insisted Ida stay indoors since she was worried about her, but Ida soon convinced her that she was strong enough to go to the fields with her sister and the boys. After living in Partschefeld for a few weeks, rumours spread about the empire's collapse. There had been no fighting in the village, no troops, no bombings, no military activity at all. Other than the occasional drone of aeroplanes passing high overhead, there was little indication that a war was taking place all around them. But no matter how high, invisible or distant the droning aeroplanes flew, the noise made the sisters nervous. Jutta and Gerhard convinced them that there was no need to run into the forest to hide each time an aeroplane passed overhead.

Soon thereafter the flights above the village increased, now coming over in daylight too, flying lower. The boys had not seen their like before. They were quickly identified as American. One day, while the boys were planting potatoes, a plane roared so low over the mountains that they threw aside their tools and ran towards the trees. As they passed an old man, he stuck out the handle of his hoe and tripped Otto, who fell face first into the dirt – Peter in turn tripped over Otto. The man told them not to run – it gave the gunners an easier target on which to train their sights. 'Stay still, motionless, invisible from above,' he advised. 'You'll be better off.'

Three days later Gerhard stood up to clean his glasses and check the progress of the other villagers scattered across the field. As he watched Peter and Otto working in an adjacent field, he saw something move on the next ridge. He squinted and put his glasses back on. A column of armoured vehicles. He knew they weren't German by their silhouettes. Radio reports had recently announced that American troops were closing in. Without thinking he shouted, 'Amis! Amis!'

Everyone jumped up and looked round to see where the American troops were. But even before anyone saw the column, they fled. In less than five minutes the village appeared abandoned. The curtains at each house were pulled tight. Within the houses a panic ensued – women digging through boxes in the attic for tablecloths, men searching for old shirts, children looking in the pantry for anything white and clean enough to use as a flag to show surrender.

Less than half an hour after Gerhard first saw the column in the distance, thirty-one white cloths fluttered in the breeze – whether neatly cut and quickly hemmed or roughly torn sheets, each hung in the highest window of every house.

They soon heard engines approaching. Ida had joined her sister after running in from the field and helping Jutta hang her flag. She had convinced Jutta to sneak with her and the children two doors up to Gerhard's house, saying that they'd be safer in a large group.

The adults crowded into the living room. The women sat stoically on the davenport, including Gerhard's wife, Susanne, and her infant son. Gerhard sat in the armchair. The boys went upstairs to keep watch. Leyna went with them, ready to run down and tell the others any news the boys could glean.

An armoured troop carrier passed the house, its top tightly sealed. A few minutes later it passed again, turned the corner and went a short distance before turning back and passing by the house a third time. The boys knew someone was inside.

steering it but saw no sign of soldiers in the vehicles or else-where. More than an hour later the same carrier crept up and back down the street. The boys grew bored, even disappointed. Since reaching Berlin the other children talked constantly about the Americans when beyond earshot of the adults. Even in Partschefeld the children had talked about them – how powerful they were, how it seemed certain that Germany would fall any day. But having watched the Russians take Germau, the boys weren't so sure that the Americans were stronger. And if stronger, they were certainly not as brave – the Russians had marched, goose-stepping all the while, into Germau without any cover at all. They had taken the village within minutes.

The boys waited, sure the Americans had something planned to redeem their meek entry. The armoured personnel carrier continued prowling the few hundred metres of road, before it finally disappeared. When they later heard it return, they knew that whatever was going to happen would happen right then – a second carrier arrived behind the first. When it came round the corner this time, the hatch on the first vehicle was opened – a soldier looked cautiously around. But instead of attacking, the two vehicles crawled here and there for another twenty minutes, until the hatch on the second one popped open and another soldier's head appeared. At that point the boys realised the soldiers were probably as bored as they were.

Otto tapped Peter's shoulder and pointed towards the junc-tion. Soldiers appeared on foot. They exchanged hand signals with those in the carriers, approached Jutta's house and knocked on the door. When no one answered they backed away, appar-ently in no mood to kick in the door and spark a possibility of house-to-house combat. Safely in the street, they signalled the other group, who repeated their comrades' actions by going to the house at the opposite end of the village and knocking on the door.

This time it opened. The Schillingers stepped out on to the porch with their hands up. Some soldiers slipped into the house and emerged with an old hunting rifle. One of them carried it to the street and handed it up to the person manning the carrier. The boys watched as the soldiers and Schillingers made exaggerated hand gestures at each other before it became clear that the soldiers didn't speak German.

The only person in Partschefeld who spoke English was the girl across the street. It was apparent that the soldiers were quick to secure this information – instead of going to the next house in an orderly manner, they came down the street to the place where Wilhelmine lived, whom the villagers called Minna for short.

Like all the village boys, Peter and Otto were smitten with Minna. They often watched her return in the afternoon from school in Rudolstadt. She was sixteen, had dark hair – which she divided in two fat, rope-like braids that hung down on either side of her head to her waist – and resembled, both boys were certain, an angel who had lost her way to heaven and ended up in Partschefeld.

When the soldiers knocked on her door, her grandfather Günter answered. More exaggerated hand gestures. Günter then turned and shouted something into the house. His wife, Brigitte, and Minna joined him on the porch. This time none of the soldiers went into the house to search it. They stood opposite the family negotiating with Günter, Minna busily translating.

At first Günter shook his head, holding his ground. But then the boys could see him starting to give in. 'Damn you!' Peter shouted, then ducked when a soldier turned towards them. When the boys again peered up over the windowsill they saw

Minna smile at the soldier conducting negotiations, then look at the ground embarrassed. A moment later they stared out of the window in disbelief, no longer paying attention to concealing themselves behind the curtain.

Minna walked through the front gate and out on to the road, with her parents on either side like chaperones, while the soldiers followed, without ever bothering to search her house, as if Minna had been promoted to commander of the invading army. The boys rolled their eyes at each other, their tell-tale expressions akin to two old men who had been through loads of wars, shaking their heads in disgust, as though they had never seen an enemy so easily duped by the oldest trick in the book. When the soldiers approached the house the boys didn't even bother to shout to Leyna to run down and warn the adults that the enemy was at the gate. They had already decided that from then on it was going to be a dog and pony show, with a handful of puppies carrying rifles, acting like they were Minna's personal bodyguards, following her around the village in her new official role as translator between the United States and the Third Reich.

Chapter 4

Gerhard had two hunting rifles that he knew the soldiers would take, but he had not expected a private from Pennsylvania to confiscate the sabre he had collected that had been used in the battle of Jena. When he objected, an officer apologised but held firm to his orders to disarm the village.

Peter could see the disappointment on Gerhard's face as he watched the soldier carry it away. But compared with the man up the street who made such a commotion that it seemed he wanted a ruling by the League of Nations before handing over his own ancient weapon, Gerhard made no complaint at all. The weapon that created the ruckus was a flintlock musket from America that no longer fired – its hammer rusted shut. Even the Americans examining it were impressed. The man's forefather had purchased it brand new after emigrating to America in the early nineteenth century but, after staying in the young republic for less than a decade, had decided he liked Europe better and came back home, carrying only the musket to remember his life abroad. It had become a cherished family heirloom, passed from generation to generation.

'Orders are orders,' the officer declared.

While the soldiers finished searching the houses, a group of village men gathered in front of Gerhard's house and

commiserated over the loss of their weapons and the conse-
quent – and abrupt – closure of the coming hunting season.
Gerhard reminded them that things could be much worse than
losing a sabre or musket. 'Amen,' they said collectively.

Much as Peter and Otto wanted to hate the Americans, especially after Minna wrapped them so easily round her finger,
they admitted that the soldiers were pretty nice. For the whole
afternoon the scent of cakes drifted throughout the village. That
evening several people threw small parties. The women had
decided the best way to keep the peace was to welcome the
guests formally. The soldiers eyed the younger women but
instead of taking the liberation of Partschefeld literally, they
minded their manners, smiled and courted them in a more
traditional manner. Their mothers kept their eyes open and
their bodies close to their daughters'. None of the soldiers spoke
German, but many had German surnames. Were it not for the
linguistic divide and the games of charades that ruled the night,
a stranger might have assumed them to be tongue-tied members
of the same culture, instead of adversaries.

A week later lightning struck the hundred-year-old tree
growing in the triangle at the middle of the village. The tree
split in two – half remained standing, the other half blocked
the road where it fell. Its upper limbs sprawled out into Jutta's
yard, near Ida's bedroom window. Ida was used to dealing with
misfortune and loss through silence, but she found it peculiar
that no one she talked to in the following days commented on
the tree that had been their central meeting place for their
entire lives. No one knew what it meant, or if it meant anything
at all, but they were superstitious enough not to dismiss it as
a random act of nature – it was an act of God, but what that
meant no one cared to guess. The men sawed down the rest of
the tree, dug up its roots to erase any visible memory of its

presence and planted a seedling in its place, whose wilting branches only drew more attention to the missing tree as far as Ida was concerned, looking out of her window as she waited each night for sleep.

She lay awake thinking about Karl, Paul and Landwirt, her mind swelling with pain at the thought of her absent family. The chores no longer provided a release, as they had in the past. Around the same time, Ida began singing to herself, folk songs, church hymns, popular songs, any whose lyrics she knew. The more songs she learned, the less she had to sing the same ones over and over. Music held boredom at bay, kept her from thinking about events she wished would float away – and sometimes the lyrics even made her smile.

Chapter 5

When the news of Berlin's fall reached Partschefeld the villagers celebrated, heartened by the thought of their husbands and sons coming home. Among themselves they began to talk about the village returning to normal, the foreigners leaving, their men returning. But at first not much changed. The Americans stayed on – even though they only passed through every few days now to check in, the villagers were tired of reporting to them. It was their village, their home. They wanted to be left in peace.

News of the men who had been away at war was slow in coming. Red Cross volunteers spread across Europe, visiting concentration camps, prisoner-of-war camps, refugee camps, cities, towns and villages, establishing the first lines of communication by recording lists filled with millions of displaced, imprisoned and deceased persons scattered across greater Europe. Millions more gathered round these constantly arriving and revised notices in hopes of finding their relatives listed among the living and if not living then at least among the recorded dead. When a familiar name did appear, letters were written and given to the local chapter to be distributed.

The first letter to reach Ida was from her father: 'I don't know why everyone was so worried about the Russians. They've treated me fine. I'm living in the same house. Germau's another matter. Our troops recaptured it sixteen times before the Russians took it for good. I don't know if any place changed hands so many times. You would think it was Berlin or Moscow by the way they fought for it. I no longer go there. In Sorgenau things are much like before the war. Different troops is all.' He asked her to write back straight away and tell him if everyone was safe.

His letter confused her. She had heard rumours that Königsberg had been so devastated when it capitulated that there were cases of cannibalism, but she had no way of knowing if these stories held any more truth than the ones she had heard of German soldiers cremating piles of German civilians with flame-throwers in Dresden and Hamburg after bombing raids had killed more civilians than anyone had the stomach to count.

The sisters wrote to Landwirt, telling him that they were in good health, were being housed in a village like Germau, apart from its location in the mountains and its miniature-sized chapel. Neither sister paid much attention to the fact that the letter went unanswered during the following months as they focused their energy on their absent husbands and, in Ida's case, son.

A short while later Ida learned that Karl was safe. The Red Cross was arranging for him to come from a village in Saxony where he had been found. They just needed to confirm his identity to ensure they didn't match the wrong people. On the afternoon Ida learned that her son would soon be with them, she hurried off to walk in the forest alone so no one would see her cry.

Instead of feeling stronger with the war ending and the news of her father's and son's survival, Ida had started to feel weaker. She couldn't tell if her weakness was the result of the burden of anxiety slowly being lifted from her shoulders, like a runner who collapses after a race, even though he has no further to run, or if her weakness lay in a physical ailment. Since the villagers had been kind enough to take care of her and the children, Ida didn't want to burden them with complaints, especially now with the news that another would be arriving. Nor did she want to burden Elsa. Besides, it was easier to put on an appearance of strength, as she had done throughout the journey. When her son returned he would need strength from her, not the other way round.

Chapter 6

The following week the entire family, along with Jutta and Gerhard, descended the mountain to meet Karl in Uhlstädt. Ida appeared calm, but everyone else was excited. They waited more than an hour before they heard the train in the distance. When it arrived, though, nothing happened quite as Ida had hoped.

Hardly a year had passed and yet he carried the sombre expression of an older man, an expression he didn't bother to alter when he and his mother first locked eyes. He stood at the top of the train's stairs, waiting for it to slow enough so he could swing down like a soldier used to travelling from one place to the next, oddly distant from his present surroundings. Ida sensed a change as soon as Karl stepped on to the platform. His initial action, his inaction rather, hurt her – in part because his expression was as she envisioned her husband's reaction would be if he ever returned from the war. Karl had lost weight. He was gaunt, but strong-looking, as if he had been doing hard physical labour. His body had matured into that of a young man and his hair was no longer neatly trimmed. After embracing, Ida tried to make him smile by introducing him to their sponsor.

'Yesterday, I showed Jutta your photograph. She thinks you could be a movie star when you grow up.'

Instead of smiling, he acted as if he had no time for her humour. For a second Ida thought she noticed a trace of suspicion in his eyes. She let the thought go, deciding she had imagined it, and wondered if it weren't she who was suspicious. She reached out a second time to hug Karl, ignoring his indifference, and held him close.

Gerhard seemed better equipped to handle Karl. Instead of hugging him like a child, Gerhard held out his hand and said, 'It's good to see a soldier returning in one piece.'

Ida could tell by the way he shrugged that Gerhard's statement had caught Karl off guard. She watched him shake Gerhard's hand, then turn to Leyna. At the sight of his little sister's beaming face his seriousness caved in. When Ida stepped forward and hugged him again, he smiled for the first time.

He tried to adjust to life in Partschefeld and even became attracted to Minna, like the other boys, but Minna paid him little attention. Whereas in Germau Karl had been the leader among the children, in Partschefeld he was just another boy. He understood that Partschefeld wasn't his village, no matter how nicely Jutta treated him. Every week other young men came home from the war.

Ida asked him only twice where his youth group had taken him and on both occasions he had ignored her question. When she heard Peter and Otto pestering him about where he had been, after telling Karl about their own journey west, she never told the younger boys to leave him alone.

Karl did eventually tell the boys what had happened, or at least part of what had happened. He had become stranded in a village somewhere in Saxony, after his youth group had fled to escape the advancing front and accidentally left him behind as he attended to cooking duties in a house they had turned into a mess hall. Since the day he had left Germau, the group leader ranted endlessly that if the Russians reached them no one would survive. He repeated it so often that the mere mention of 'Ivan' – as they often referred to the Russians, in a manner similar to the way that the Russians referred to them as 'Fritz' – made the boys tremble, their bodies filling with adrenalin and fear, as they fell, when ordered, into their practised defensive manoeuvres by which they were taught to defend the Fatherland against Ivan to their death.

Karl's youth group had become so small by that time that when the group fled, the remaining fourteen members had piled into the back of a single truck, which had raced out of the village before Karl realised the Russians were approaching. The sole Party member in the village, a man wearing a perfectly tailored Nazi uniform, stepped out of his house to stand sentry in the centre of the village.

As Karl ran in his direction to ask where everyone had gone, he heard the grinding gears of a vehicle, followed by doors slamming. Knowing something was amiss, Karl turned back and ran towards the house. Before reaching its door, he heard gunshots. He turned and saw the sentry fall to the ground.

He went into the house and shouted to the villagers gathered in the cellar as a barrage of artillery erupted. It rained with such force that it seemed the world itself was about to cave in. In all his months moving across Poland and into Saxony he had never come under direct fire. But even greater than the fear of the bombs themselves was his fear of the Russian soldiers who he was certain would soon enter the village and cut out his tongue, leaving him to die on the ground.

He tumbled down the steps into the cellar as shells exploded above, the noise so loud, the repercussions shaking the ground so great, that a deafening silence enveloped him. Artillery continued pounding the village, though he could no longer judge the duration as time lost all meaning – its void, the eternity bridging life and death, that tiny, one-way gap between the two, whose narrow split when fully crossed became irrevocable and irreversible so that whether or not life continued surviving on the other side, no such knowledge could ever be passed backwards. Bombs exploded in every direction, rumbling through the ground to the women and children huddled in the cellar. The atmosphere reeked of death – the perspiration dripping down Karl's face, the silence between each shell as they waited for the next, the baby screaming beside him held tightly in its mother's arms, the shell they had been waiting for that finally hit, collapsing the roof, which fell down all the way to the kitchen floor through which an enormous beam came crashing, sticking into the earthen wall of the cellar just beside Karl's head like a giant spear violently thrust from the sky.

When the artillery ceased, Karl was unable to stop shaking. The women and children were now silent. Even the baby had stopped screaming. In an attempt to gain control of his body, to prove to himself that he was still alive, he stood up. The woman beside him winced, as though his standing was more of a shock than the shells that had been pounding the village. He struggled among the debris towards the fractured stairs leading to the kitchen. When he freed the door, light flooded into the cellar. The kitchen was no longer inside the house. It no longer existed. In its place lay a pile of splintered beams. Karl climbed over the ruins until he was standing where the front door had been.

In a daze, he wandered on to the pockmarked road, dust and smoke wafting all around him. He walked across the square where he had seen the man shot before the shelling had started, no longer caring if another fusillade began. Most of the buildings had been hit. Flames were spreading from one structure to the next. Karl thought for the first time in weeks about Germau and whether or not his own parents' shop was still standing, then he heard an engine like the one he had heard before the shelling began. His recently acquired calm, a state of temporary shock that had allowed him to walk unperturbed through the destroyed village, gave way to panic. He fled towards the trees. As soon as he reached them, he hid behind the first tree large enough to shield himself and waited for the Russians.

Karl bowed his head and prayed, accepting the conclusion his group leader had drilled into his mind that he would soon die. He wasn't prepared to defend the village, no longer possessed the will to defend anything, or even cared about his own life. After reciting a prayer, he inhaled, lifted his head and peered out from behind the tree. The sight shocked him almost as much as the recent shelling.

The jeep pulling into the village was filled with American soldiers. Americans had shelled them, not Russians. For over a month, several of the boys in his group had whispered hopes among themselves to be able to surrender to the Americans, having heard that their lives would be spared in such an event. Despite the fact that they had just tried to kill him, the sight of the Americans filled him with so much relief that he swore to God in a quickly improvised prayer that if they treated him as fairly as the boys in his group had secretly whispered they would, he would commit himself to the United States with the same devotion he had committed himself to the Third Reich. Later that afternoon Karl learned that the other fourteen boys and their leader, who had managed to escape the village, were killed when one of the shells fired by the Americans hit and obliterated their escape vehicle.

Chapter 7

A few months after the Americans occupied Partschefeld they made preparations to pull out. The village became rife with anxiety at the news of the American withdrawal – they weren't being freed, just passed from one occupying force to the next. They felt betrayed by the Americans. Secret arrangements had been made. New borders were to divide what remained of the country among Russia, Britain, France and the United States. The villagers had become comfortable with the Americans. Now they became fearful with the announcement that the Russians would soon replace them.

Regardless of Landwirt's reasonable opinion of the Russians in Samland, Ida had had personal experiences with those same forces. She knew that her contact had been during conquest, whereas now the Russians were entering as a peacetime force, but such rationalising did little to reduce her anxiety. The Americans assured them that they would be treated respectfully, no matter who administered them. Minna and her grandparents were upset – Minna since it meant she'd lose her distinction as the village translator and her grandparents out of fear that the incoming Russian soldiers' inevitable attraction to her might not prove as benign as the Americans'.

Their initial arrival, though, wasn't as traumatic as the

villagers had anticipated. Only a few bothered to check on the village and then only on weekdays. Unlike the tongue-tied Americans, who shared an ethnic affinity but limited cultural sophistication with the villagers, several Russians spoke fluent German and had a complex understanding of German culture. One even appeared grateful he had been stationed there. He loved music and played on the organ in the village chapel a number of pieces Liszt had composed at his former home nearby.

The villagers expressed appreciation at the Russian soldier's knowledge of the arts that had once flourished in the region, but inside they were intimidated: he had a greater grasp of their regional history than anyone in the village. He had an advanced academic degree for which he had written his thesis on the Weimar Republic.

At first few villagers complained out loud after the Americans relinquished the territory, but over time their voices rose. They were now required to keep strict records of all stored food and production levels for the Russian administrators; residents could keep only enough to feed themselves at subsistence levels – the rest was shipped elsewhere by the new Communist government. They were used to sending out food during the war, but when there was a surplus from the harvest or an extra hog that didn't go to market, they kept it for their own consumption. The new policies forbade this. Furthermore, they were required to produce a certain amount of food, more than they had ever consistently done in the past. If they failed to maintain their quotas or were caught trying to keep a part of the harvest, they faced intimidation or arrest.

These pressures changed the village dynamics to such a degree that many younger residents now made plans to move to other regions, further west, as soon as restrictions on relocation were eased. One wanted to move to Berlin and another to Hamburg, instead of maintaining the farms that had been in their families for generations.

Chapter 8

A few weeks later, when walking in from the fields together, Karl told his mother that he felt as if time had started to pass faster since the war ended. For some, infantrymen in particular, it was the opposite: time dragged with the close of war, as the rush that had accompanied their survival during combat receded into a civilian life that, by contrast, carried few risks at all. But for Karl and his mother the slow passage of time they had experienced during the war became more brisk with peace. Time passed with such alacrity that even though neither wanted the dreadful slowness they had experienced wanting the war to end, both wished separately that time would slow down enough to allow them to take comfort in the fact that they were still alive and in good health.

However that was only part of the problem: at least in Ida's case – she wasn't in good health. She hid it from herself, denied it, refused to acknowledge that anything could be wrong, even though she had felt weaker in the months, which soon passed into a half-year, since the war had ended. But she was never so weak as to be unable to carry out her chores. She refused to let exhaustion keep her from working like everyone else.

But no matter how much Ida tried to distract herself, something was wrong. She sometimes stopped in the middle of a walk and closed her eyes to gather strength or harness an unspoken pain. When her children asked what was wrong, she answered, 'Woman's illness,' rubbing her belly to demonstrate that the abdomen, the womb, formed the centremost part of a woman's body. 'It's nothing. Stop worrying your little heads. It'll keep you from growing.'

Then the letter arrived nearly a year after the surrender from Jiera, Landwirt's wife. 'I'm not sure how to begin,' she had begun. 'I have news that must reach you.' She said she was going back to Lithuania, but that wasn't the reason she was writing. It was the first time they had heard from Landwirt or her since the original letter had arrived months before, when Landwirt had written that he was being treated well. Jiera's letter, though, carried different news.

As the winter following the capture of the peninsula set in, food became scarce. With few rations, the new government first allocated supplies to its own soldiers ostensibly defending the peninsula. Leftovers went to the citizens of Königsberg. There was little left to distribute to the natives in the countryside.

Jiera said that she and Landwirt had agreed it was best for her to go to Königsberg alone to find food for them. They were weak with hunger by the time she left for the capital. Winter had set in. They had kept the fire burning with turf, but there was nothing left to cook. Finding food in the capital was harder than Jiera had thought it would be. A week after arriving she had secured a small cache, having become intimate with a guard – a Karelian from a northern territory that had recently been exchanged between the Finns and the Russians. He and Jiera had met at a tavern and became friendly over their hushed discussion one night about living under the Russians now instead of the Germans. She carried the food back to Sorgenau, hitching rides on army trucks that travelled constantly between

Königsberg and Pillau. At the junction in Fischhausen another truck took her north near the ruins of Germau – which the Russians had since renamed Pycckoe.

Landwirt was nowhere to be found when she got to Sorgenau. The ashes in the fireplace were cold. She went from house to house – most inhabited by soldiers. After asking everyone she finally learned from the official overseeing the village that he had died a few days earlier and had been buried in an unmarked grave. She didn't bother to ask his cause of death – she knew: starvation. Like many other older Samlanders who lacked skills that the new administrators needed, natives who had stayed behind in their ancestral villages, hoping that their old age, the fact that they posed no threat, would assure their safety. 'I'm sorry,' Jiera concluded. 'I still love him. He talked often about his family. He's in a better place now.'

Ida set down the letter. She tried to recollect Landwirt's expression on the morning she had last seen him. He had made the painful confession on that occasion that he had no power to defend her or the children – said she and the children could move faster without him and that their chances of survival were better travelling alone than with him. Ida picked up the letter again. She wasn't so much shocked as saddened – now both her parents were gone. Of all the ways her father might have died, she would never have guessed starvation. Hobbling about on his wooden leg, he seemed too strong, too stubborn, too tenacious to die in such a feeble way. His death forced Ida to face the reality that the life she had known on the peninsula had been swallowed whole in a single year. It was no longer a simple matter of not being able to go home again: home no longer existed.

Chapter 9

After Ida learned of her father's death, news arrived in Partschefeld on a regular basis telling of missing fathers, husbands and sons as if a dam had burst at the Red Cross headquarters in Switzerland, flooding the names and locations of the living and the dead across Germany.

Ida's husband, Paul, was found in a British garrison, where he was being held, serving as camp cook. Elsa's husband, Konrad, was in a Russian prison camp, also listed as uninjured. The sisters wrote to their husbands. Elsa wrote seven or eight letters before she heard from Konrad almost six months later. He was being moved among prison camps, the mail either lagging behind or not being delivered at all.

Paul was faster in responding, his situation more stable near Hanover. But instead of receiving a letter from him delighted to have found his family, Ida sensed a dismissive tone when he said that he had not expected to learn that they were stuck in the Russian zone. Ida, self-conscious about her experiences, felt his tone implied that most women in the Russian sector had been violated at one point or another.

She knew her husband well enough to interpret the subtle but snide tone he could insert into a single sentence or turn of phrase, as if he were standing over her, talking down to her.

After all the hardships she had endured, she was astonished, more angry than hurt, that he was still capable of maintaining that arrogant part of his personality she had always despised. She was hurt even more by what his allusion to the Russians implied – that as long as she was stuck in the Russian sector, he wouldn't risk coming to visit after the British released him for fear of being stuck there himself. Her hope that if Paul had survived, his experiences during the war would have changed him, made him see life in a different, more agreeable, generous and optimistic light if for no other reason than he had survived a conflict that had ruthlessly killed so many others, was fast diminishing.

Before she wrote back, she accepted that the family life she had dreamed about as a young woman, which for a brief time early in their marriage had been realised, was not likely to re-emerge. Through war and now peace Paul remained the same – self-centred, arrogant and unconcerned with anything but his own well-being. She decided that the fact that her children were with her was enough – she could find happiness in their joys, whether or not she had a partner to help raise them.

Though it angered her, she understood Paul's interpretation of the Russian zone. There was a hierarchy of preference for civilians and returning soldiers alike. It varied, depending on where each person was originally from. While most ancestral residents of Partschefeld preferred to be in the American zone, their first loyalty lay to their village. Refugees from the east, who had lost their homes and thus had no loyalty to any region of the truncated Germany, preferred first the American and British zones, the French zone second and the Russian last. The French and Russian zones were the less desired because rumours spread, both unfounded and confirmed, that the French and Russians were more prone to use their position as an occupying force by abusing and, in some cases, starving Germans, particularly German prisoners of war, in personal and private acts of retribution for the violence they and their families had experienced under German occupation. Many refugees from the east who had fled west had tried to get to the British or American zone before the surrender was formally signed.

Refugees pouring in from central and eastern Europe tended to see the war as one between Germany and Russia. To them the Soviet-German War was so large and devastating that its disappearance from public debate after the surrender shocked them. They understood that their plight was fast becoming invisible, their private struggles as unnoticed as the uncounted millions of Russians, Belarusians, Poles, Ukrainians, Romanians, Yugoslavs and other ethnic groups who had no nations at all along the Eastern Front, where more anonymous individuals, soldiers and civilians alike, of every background imaginable, perished between 1941 and 1945 than in any military conflict in human history.

But no matter how deafening the silence, Ida's goal was to make sure her family stayed together. When Paul wrote a month later, telling her he would be released from the garrison in that spring of 1946, Ida knew he had no intention of returning to her and the children. He had made plans to go down to Goslar, a medieval town at the foot of the Harz Mountains, where other refugees had settled. He had a number of contacts through an emerging East Prussian underground who had agreed to lend him backing for a new business. He had stated in one letter, which Ida found offensive, that East Prussians might have lost their homes and their land, but they hadn't lost their wits or ability to organise. She found the statement offensive because his tone implied the war had never ended, was simply idling for a time, while the conquerors moved the population around as they tried to figure out how to merge the numerous different cultures they were slowly realising existed under the German tongue.

The first letters Ida had received from him were sent through the Red Cross – but his subsequent letters, written while still in the garrison, were hand-carried by fellow East Prussians who had developed their own courier service to get round the officials who sometimes read and censored mail. In one letter he wrote that the influx of refugees in Goslar could easily support another delicatessen, especially one whose owner knew the delicacies people liked best.

The idea made perfect sense, but she knew, as he knew, that it would be almost impossible for her and the children to get permission to move. Families were brought together but the authorities would in all likelihood, and logically, insist that Paul move to the Russian zone in which his family had already settled. After all, he hadn't even established residency in Goslar.

But in the letters that followed, Paul persuaded Ida to let Karl join him there to launch the shop. He said it was easy for children to sneak between the zones. Paul was due to be released next month. He was eager to set up shop. With the limited capital he had been promised, he needed his son's free labour, along with that of any apprentices he could find, to make up for his slim budget.

Karl told Ida he wanted to go. He had never felt accepted by the villagers, as his siblings and mother had. Ultimately, she agreed for a number of reasons: it was important for him to have a male role model with whom he had a familial connection; it was necessary for him to learn a trade; she and the children needed money, a stipulation to which Paul and Karl had agreed. But had she wanted him to stay, she knew he wouldn't have. He had already resolved that life would be better in Goslar, he had told her. She knew, too, that he thought the move would let him escape something he had been through that he still refused to articulate.

Chapter 10

Nothing worked out as planned. Before Karl had even helped his father finish the construction of the shop, before he had butchered a single side of meat to begin his apprenticeship, Paul decided his son lacked the natural talent to become a master butcher. He traded him to be apprenticed at a local bakery in exchange for a small sum of money the baker had secretly promised beforehand, money Paul needed to buy scales and a cash register for the grand opening. The baker sent Paul one of his own apprentices, who he likewise claimed lacked any natural talent for baking; in fact, the baker disliked the boy, a Catholic, since he insisted on being permitted to attend church each Sunday, the busiest day of the week.

His father's rejection hurt Karl, but it had been so long since they had lived together that Paul no longer seemed much like a father anyway. Karl decided he had never wanted to be a butcher. He had never wanted to be a baker either but a baker was better than a butcher since the kitchen smelled of butter and was kept warm in the winter.

Despite the trouble with his father, Karl liked Goslar. It had been spared bombings, its town square was made from different coloured cobbles that radiated outwards like rays of the sun from the fountain at the centre. Kaiserpfalz, the former Imperial

Palace at the edge of the town, built in 1050, was in perfect condition, with its statue of the Emperor Frederick Barbarossa on horseback defiantly guarding the entrance, as though he had never perished in the river leading the crusaders to Palestine or been associated with Operation Barbarossa, Hitler's delusion of turning the entire continent of Europe into an immense German state. Unlike so many others, the statue had never been toppled after the Nazi defeat – but only because the Russians had never made it this far west, Karl knew. The eastern offensive launched in Barbarossa's honour had not affected the British and Americans as much. But regardless of how much Karl liked Goslar, one aspect bothered him: he had come here to try to distance himself from war memories. Instead of succeeding, however, the presence of so many refugees constantly reminded him of the war. At least in Partschefeld his family had been the only refugees – in Goslar they filled entire neighbourhoods.

Karl only saw his father once or twice a week, even though he lived just a few blocks away. Before Karl had been traded to his new job, Paul had told the baker that his son needed four days off at the end of each month so that he could see his mother. This was his father's way, Karl knew, of keeping his agreement with Ida and using him to deliver money to a black-market slaughterhouse in Weimar that delivered inexpensive meat to Paul on reciept of payment.

Karl soon fell into the habit of sneaking across the border on the last weekend of every month, following footpaths worn into the mountainside by smugglers crossing zones. Once deep inside Thuringia, he emerged from the forest and hitched rides. He first visited his mother for a night, giving her some money, then travelled back to Weimar, where he paid the contact, who then sent runners carrying the goods across the border. His father didn't care who made the deliveries, Karl knew, but he only trusted blood relatives to carry the money. Sometimes the contact loaded Karl up with butcher knives manufactured in the east that Paul sold to other butchers, especially apprentices – including his own – on credit. His father had numerous small-scale schemes, like many refugees who had lost everything, to help keep business profitable. One night Karl met another boy his age sneaking across the Harz Mountains, who told him that the Russians had kept Buchenwald running to imprison Nazis.

'The war's over,' Karl said, not believing the concentration camp was still open.

'Go and see for yourself.'

Next month Karl came to a 'Y' in the path and went right, instead of left to the road. He crept through the forest until he came to the edge of a clearing, where buildings and fences stood. He could see people moving. He became frightened and ran along a fence near the back of the prison. As he searched for the path off the mountain he came upon bodies piled in the forest and a trench that was being dug to bury them. Freshly turned earth with shovels stuck in the soil lined one side. He looked around but saw no one. Without waiting for anyone to return, he ran as fast as he could into the trees and did not stop until he came to a road down in the valley more than an hour later.

He began to have nightmares about his own imprisonment and death. The anxiety he had experienced during the war returned to fever pitch, for he was terrified he might be caught and imprisoned in Buchenwald. At such moments he knew it was impossible to forget what had happened after he left home, but instead of facing his past, he rationalised it by diverting his thoughts to other crimes that were still being committed, which no one cared to acknowledge.

When he reached his mother the day he had been to

Buchenwald, Ida could sense his anxiety. Though silent when he first got there, he later blurted out that he had seen men left to be buried in the forest. His mother listened patiently.

At first, Ida kept quiet to let him calm down. She knew it was her responsibility to help Karl see the world in the way he had seen it prior to his indoctrination in the Hitler Youth. 'If they had never set up those camps,' she finally said, 'those men wouldn't be there now. They must face the consequences.' She paused for a few seconds. 'You can only ignore the past for so long.' Her words subtly urged him to share his war experiences with her. When he didn't reply, she took his hand and led him to the village chapel.

As soon as he saw where she was taking him he thought of Mr Wolff – the lessons he had taught him and the icy road on which he had found his body at dawn. He tried to shut out the image but the dead man persisted, refusing to be dismissed so easily.

At first he felt sad, but as they walked down the road, his sadness turned to guilt, then self-hate. He remembered his last talk with Mr Wolff, when he had suggested that Karl be cautious of people who forced their ideas on him. Karl felt himself transported back to the vestry in Germau, listening to Mr Wolff, before the sight of his murdered body returned. He tried to force it from his mind but each time he succeeded he was confronted by another memory – his leader screaming at him in the forest, a boy curled up on the ground, then a column of Jewish prisoners being marched across the Polish countryside. Karl stopped in the middle of the road and let go of his mother. He covered his face with his hands, hoping to slow the images now flooding his mind – the boy stared relentlessly into his eyes – but the harder Karl tried to forget, the deeper the mem-ories etched themselves.

He looked up at his mother. She was right: the road to freedom lay in confronting his past. But each time he tried to speak, he became so nervous he couldn't get a single word out. He was frightened – she might think differently of him. Would she still love him?

'What's wrong?' Ida asked.

Karl pretended not to hear.

'Tell me what you're thinking.'

Karl looked away.

'You must tell me!' She could see him trembling; then, without waiting, she asked, 'Did you have anything to do with it?'

'With what?'

'You know what I'm talking about.'

'I swear, I don't.'

'The girls who were killed in Palmnicken. Did you help the mayor?'

Karl didn't know what she was talking about. His thoughts shifted to Mr Wolff again and to the girls murdered on the road to Palmnicken. 'I didn't help anybody,' he said.

'Damn it, Karl! Tell me the truth!' she said, starting to cry.

'I'm telling you. I never went to Palmnicken. I never did anything to any girls.'

'You swear to God you're telling the truth?' She looked into his eyes.

'I'm telling you the truth!' His thoughts now veered to a grove of trees, his group leader screaming; the boy's eyes staring into his; adrenalin coursing through his veins.

'You swear you didn't have anything to do with the girls?'

'I told you,' he said. 'I swear.'

Now is the time, he said to himself, trying to build up the courage.

But before he had a chance to say anything else, his mother pulled him to her and clutched him tightly. 'I'm sorry,' she said.

He felt a tear, then another, fall on to his face and slide down his cheek from his mother's eyes looking down at him. He started to cry with her. It was too late now to say anything. He couldn't hurt her more. He would have to wait.

Chapter 11

After they left the chapel, Karl asked if he could help Gerhard, who had been the only one to treat him like a man when he first arrived in Partschefeld. If there was anyone in the village besides his mother Karl could talk with, Gerhard was the one.

When he got to the barn, Gerhard signalled for Karl to join him hauling feed to the shed. Karl tried to think of a way to broach the subject. He had to talk to someone. For more than an hour, as he built up his courage, he decided it would be best to ask Gerhard first about his thoughts on Buchenwald.

'Never heard of it,' Gerhard answered.

'The prison above Weimar,' Karl clarified. 'Where the Jews were.'

Gerhard looked at him blankly, as though he had no idea what he was talking about, and continued working without comment. Even if he hadn't known during the war, Karl thought, he had to have heard about it since the war ended. Everyone knew there was a big prison there. Karl realised then that any questions about the war were unwelcome. Chagrined, he helped Gerhard finish the work, aware that if he intended to face his past he would have to do so alone and in silence.

Several months later Karl decided to ask his father to come with him on one of the trips, to surprise Ida. His parents hadn't seen each other since 1941. He knew it was unlikely, but much as he resented his father, he sometimes fantasised about his parents being together. The idea of seeing them with one another would make it feel as it had been before the war, before everything had happened. The first few times Karl had visited his mother she had asked about Paul and even told him to say hello. But on subsequent visits, when Karl carried no reply from his father, she stopped asking. One evening when he picked up the money to carry to Paul's contact in Weimar, Karl took a deep breath and said, 'Come with me. Peter and Leyna miss you.'

'I'm too busy,' Paul said and changed the subject: 'I have a meeting with the Laufers to talk about opening another shop in Hanover.'

When Karl saw his mother the next day, he didn't tell her that he had asked Paul to come. He wanted to, so she knew that he had tried to surprise her by bringing the family together, but he didn't want to hurt her. Instead of talking about Paul, he told her about Goslar and how he never went up to the park any more since the local kids often fought with him when they heard his East Prussian accent. Ida consoled him by saying that people talked differently everywhere, that there would always be people who wouldn't like his accent no matter where he lived: 'If we moved back to Germau, nobody would like your accent there, either.'

Karl laughed at his mother's joke. He often worried about her, but realised that she would be fine if she could joke so freely about the new residents who now lived in Samland who didn't speak a word of German. It was dawning on him that it didn't matter where he lived. He would probably live in many more places before he finally settled in any one of them. He sometimes thought about America too, but it wasn't possible to leave the country. Immigration was compulsory for most refugees and emigration was not permitted, except in rare cases where one possessed a refined scientific skill that America could use to bolster its own military strength, such as Wernher von Braun's talent in developing the V-2 missiles that the German army had rained on London towards the end of the war. After spending the war at a secret base on the Baltic coast as director of the German Rocket Research Centre, von Braun was admitted straight into the United States after the surrender, where he became advisor to America's burgeoning missile programme in New Mexico, while most of the other refugees from his home town, now in Poland, who lacked the military skills desired by the Americans were forced into Germany.

Karl dismissed any thought of returning to Samland or Masuria after hearing rumours from the refugees in Goslar. A few East Prussians, including his uncle, in Masuria – the southern part of the former territory given to Poland – had stayed behind to manage the public works for the Polish administrators, who were busy learning the systems the Germans had built over the previous centuries. He had not heard anything negative from his uncle but many who stayed behind fared no better than Landwirt.

A Samlander his father had introduced him to, who had escaped from a train headed for Siberia, told Karl that it was over. The peninsula that had given birth to Immanuel Kant and his *Critique of Pure Reason* had been turned on its head. Kant, who never left Samland, even at the height of his fame, was said to be missing from his tomb. The Russian government, fearing an uprising, was systematically cleansing the peninsula of its German past and erecting barbed-wire fences to seal its borders. In the process they had also unwittingly expelled the few indigenous Balt-Prussians who had assimilated into the previous conquerer's culture. The Russians were working as hard as possible to erase any evidence of the past, except for a few young German girls, who had married Russian soldiers who had protected them from other Russian soldiers during the fall of Königsberg.

Chapter 12

Apart from the weakness and slight pain Ida felt in her lower abdomen, there was little indication that anything was wrong. At least not that anyone could tell by the way Ida carried herself, as strong and independent as always. When Karl visited her again in September the only thing he noticed was how much she had fallen in love with a new song. Still unable to work up the courage to discuss the events gnawing at his insides, he concentrated instead on her voice. She loved the song so much that she had even made Karl learn a verse so they could sing it together. He refused at first, embarrassed, but when he saw how much it meant to her he turned back towards the village to make sure no one was within earshot, then committed the lines to memory as they walked and sang in unison, laughing each time Karl fell out of tune.

The event stood out in Karl's mind not so much because of her infatuation with a song that let her imagine she was in love again in a small island on the coast of the warm Mediterranean, but because his mother seemed happier than at any time he could recall since they had been reunited after leaving Germau, as though she were finally allowing herself the luxury of acknowledging that she had accomplished her main goal: ensuring her children's safe survival. He thought about the way she had laughed and sung like a girl falling in love for the first time. In fact, his mother wasn't the only one falling in love during that first lean year after occupation, when it seemed half of Germany's population wished they lived anywhere but in Germany, a sentiment expressed through the popularity of that first hit after the surrender that carried girls' minds who dreamed of being in love away from German soil down to Capri, where cute Italian boys working the fishing boats wooed them on the beaches late at night, where shoulder straps fell as they wrapped their arms round each other, their nationalities melding in the gentle motions of love.

Karl glanced around to make sure no one was watching, then slipped across the border into the British sector, and smiled, thinking about his mother, remembering the time she had taken him and his little brother up to Rauschen when he was a small boy. Their father had been away on business. Instead of inviting the family to come with him, Paul had promised to go fishing while away and bring enough sweetwater fish back so they could have a fish fry. Even though Karl was only seven at the time, he still remembered his mother's hurt expression as they watched the train carry his father away. It was the first time he had been consciously aware that one person could affect another's emotions and he remembered it all the more since the person being affected was his mother.

But Karl also remembered that she hadn't stayed sad for long. After walking home that morning, she had made plans to rent a room near the beach in Rauschen for the weekend, so they could go on their own. She had even promised Karl that he could go to the pier and fish as much as he liked. He had grinned when he had seen his mother try to hide her own smile that morning. Karl promised her not to tell his father anything about their weekend at the beach. It would be their own little secret, the first real promise of any consequence Karl ever made. His mother had told the neighbours that she was taking the children to see her parents. The first thing she did after they reached Rauschen that afternoon was walk the boys down to the beach, where she bought herself some amber earrings from one of the jewellers who erected display cases on the boardwalk. The earrings caught and held the light of the setting sun in their small dangling globes, hanging on both sides of his mother's face, which he looked up at as she fiddled with the clasps until she noticed him staring at her and bent down to kiss his forehead. Later that night, after his brother had fallen asleep, she had asked him to come and lie on the bed with her. They had talked late into the night, then fallen asleep in each other's arms.

In the same way he had become aware the first time of his mother's disappointment and her ability to overcome it, Karl now realised all these years later that he couldn't let others, such as his father, influence his emotions. His mind flashed briefly to his group leader screaming, who he now understood had influenced him so much that he had let his emotions rule his actions. But before he completed the thought, he refocused on his father to distract himself. He'd take the money to Weimar, he told himself, but only because it gave him a chance to visit his mother. The following month, however, he had to skip going to Partschefeld in order to take exams for his apprenticeship. He had started attending baking school in the evenings to earn his credentials, so he could find work anywhere in Germany.

One afternoon when he sat down to write a short note to his mother telling her that he was unable to find a copy of *Grimm's Fairy Tales* – the Allies had recently banned them, fearing they had contributed to Nazi brutality – which she had asked him to send to his younger siblings, Karl was interrupted by the owner of the bakery. He came to the attic where Karl lived and handed him a letter from Elsa. It instructed him to hurry back with his father. Ida had been taken to the hospital in Jena. For a second Karl thought it might be a clever joke his mother was playing to get the family together, but he soon decided that Elsa's insistence that he hurry was not a joke at all. Karl ran across town to find his father.

When he found him, his father said he had received a letter too and had just finished writing a reply, which lay on the desk to be posted the next morning. Karl glanced at the letter, stunned at its words: 'The hospital will take care of her. There's little we can do. She's been through a lot. Now isn't the time to panic. Let her rest a little, then we'll come.'

As Karl finished reading, his father scolded him for being too emotional, like his mother, saying that Ida and her sister always jumped to the worst possible conclusion whenever anything happened. 'They're all the same,' Paul continued, speaking of women in general. 'Keep your chin up. Everything will be fine. We'll go to see her as soon as I save a little money, in case we have to pay bribes to get back across the border.'

Karl listened obediently without revealing the apprehension simmering in his mind. When his father finished Karl turned, without saying a word, and left the shop. He stood briefly out front as rays of sun broke through the cloud cover. Changing from the person he was in the shop listening to his father and into another out on the pavement, he had been granted the privilege of viewing his actions from afar: watching the stranger on the street, all the familial, emotional and cultural inhibitions he had been conditioned to fell away magically as he watched himself leave the kerb and cross the street. Paul came out and shouted at him as he turned the corner without looking back and disappeared from his father's view.

He felt as if an equilibrium had been disrupted, as if he had entered an inverted state of vertigo in which he wasn't dizzy at all – on the contrary, he had never felt more firm-footed than at that moment. His perception of the world – consensual reality and all its unwritten axioms, laws and rules that he had adhered to without ever questioning them – peeled away like the skin of a butchered chicken tossed into a pot of boiling water, the flesh beneath the surface suddenly becoming the surface itself, the world converging as all the knowledge he had gathered up to that point began to coalesce into the single profound realisation that he was free to do what he must, regardless of what any form of authority dictated. He ran to the bakery, climbed the stairs to the attic, gathered his clothes into a bag and left Goslar without telling his father.

Chapter 13

After catching a ride out of town towards the Russian zone, he was dropped off near the edge of the forest. Entering the trees, he experienced a profound loneliness. He thought about his mother's repeated attempts to make him confront his past. The happiness, or at least respite, he had hoped his move would provide had failed. Even if he stayed in Goslar to finish his apprenticeship, his original desire to be near his father had gone. Not only did he no longer want to be near him, he didn't want to be anything like him – his father ignored parts of his life as though they didn't exist: his wife, his children. He thought only of himself and his future – unburdened by his past. Despite breaking free from his father, Karl knew he had to confront his own past. His mood darkened when he acknowledged that he would never be able to disassociate himself completely from what he had done.

He thought again about first seeing Buchenwald and his brief talk with his mother, when she had taken him to the chapel; the forced silence he had experienced afterwards trying to talk with Gerhard. His mind shifted to his early childhood, playing on the hill above Germau, in an attempt to block the images that kept flashing into his head. As had been the case each time before, the more he resisted the memories, the more immediate they became, until the part of his life he had tried to forget flooded his mind – memories that for the first time since the event he didn't try to stop.

The deeper he walked into the forest, following a path illuminated by the moon, the further back his memories travelled until he could feel the cold air against his face on the morning he had stood beside his mother on the platform outside Germau. Everything that had happened in the following months occurred in such a chaotic manner that he no longer remembered with any clarity all the places he had been on the journey. Initially, the group advanced towards the border to help fortify a defence, but as they were crossing Poland the leader stopped several times to offer their services to scattered SS demolition squads.

One afternoon he was dropped off to help clean up a compound. He was told to haul timbers away from the foundation of an outbuilding, then cover it with sticks and leaves to make it look like the remnant of an abandoned structure that had been there before the war. While doing so, his group leader approached him quietly from behind and shouted. Karl jumped.

He began ridiculing Karl: 'You'll never make it through the war. A coward like you deserves whatever you have coming.' The leader ranted for nearly half an hour until Karl felt weak from the verbal assault. Afterwards, Karl watched him walk to the edge of the clearing and step into the brush to relieve himself. The leader shouted for him to come and help him lift something. Karl walked cautiously towards him. When he neared the undergrowth, he saw that instead of zipping up his pants after urinating, his leader stood exposing himself. At first Karl tried to look away, but the leader stopped him and looked straight into his eyes. 'What are you scared of, little girl?'

Karl didn't care what he called him – he wanted only to get it over with as fast as possible. As they were standing there, a twig cracked nearby. The leader frantically zipped up his pants. They hid for several minutes. He then motioned for Karl to follow. Within a few metres they passed through an opening in the undergrowth and entered a grove of trees. His leader studied the ground, before focusing on an area that had been trampled near the trunk of a massive tree. He motioned for Karl to stay put, then swung wide round the tree to cut off the escape route. As he moved forward, he pulled his pistol from its holster. He went only ten or fifteen steps and froze, staring at something behind the tree that apparently had not seen him.

He quietly retreated a few steps and waved Karl to him. He raised the gun in his right hand, grabbed its barrel with his left and let go of the handle, which he now held out for Karl to take. Karl hesitated, unsure what he was supposed to do. His leader thrust the handle towards him. This time Karl grabbed it. Confused, he looked at the gun in his hand, then at his leader, whose attention had now returned to the tree. Karl gripped the handle in his right hand, as he had been taught a few months earlier, slid his finger round the trigger and pointed it at the tree trunk.

The leader glanced back to make sure he was in position. He then launched himself round the tree, surprising his prey, and dragged into view a boy whose collar he clutched so tightly that Karl heard him choke.

When he released him, the barrel of the pistol Karl held was pointed at the boy's head. In a state of shock he had not lowered the gun. He glanced at his leader. He had planned it this way, he realised, when his leader grinned at him.

The boy cowered and avoided eye contact. Moisture spread from his crotch. Karl saw a tattered yellow Star of David sewn to his shirt. They were the same age. Karl's hands started shaking. He realised what the leader wanted him to do. He lowered the barrel of the gun until it no longer pointed at the boy's head.

In disgust, the leader kicked the boy in the chest. Everything seemed to click into slow motion. A dull thud filled the forest as the boot made contact. A loud shriek followed – air forced from the boy's lungs. He had kicked him so hard that a trickle of blood spilled from his mouth.

'You piece of shit,' the leader screamed. 'Pull the trigger, you Jew-loving pig!' He kicked the boy again.

Karl's body tightened, including his hands, until all the tension was focused on his index finger.

'You're scared! You couldn't kill a Jew if you wanted to.'

He taunted Karl, screaming that he and the boy would be buried together if he didn't follow orders.

At that second all Karl wanted to do was go home. He could see the village lights as he crested the hill coming back at night from school in Pillau. Fog rolled in from the sea. Karl shivered. Then started to cry. He stopped himself. He didn't want his mother to see him crying.

His leader started to scream something, then stopped.

The boy, now curled up on the ground, muttered something.

When the leader realised the boy was praying, he started screaming at Karl again.

Karl tried to discern the boy's calm words. In the short pauses during which his leader caught his breath before screaming more orders, Karl recognised that the boy's words sounded vaguely familiar. He was praying in Hebrew.

The leader reached out to take the gun.

Karl jerked away.

'Are you going to stand there like an idiot and let this para-site survive?'

Karl's diaphragm constricted. He couldn't breathe. His head felt as though it were bursting. He glanced at the boy. Right then, he identified more with him than with his leader. He could have sworn he could feel the boy's emotions. He didn't want to. He didn't want to feel anything. He became enraged. He wanted silence. The only lucid thought he could harness was to make the world around him go quiet.

The boy suddenly looked up and made eye contact. At the same time Karl's leader tried to grab the gun.

Karl panicked. He stepped beyond the leader's reach – furious that he had tried to take the gun. He glanced down at the boy – enraged at his subtle gesture. Their eyes locked.

'Your mother's probably sucking Ivan's dick this second!'

Karl tensed. His body arched. His eyes shut.

An explosion ripped through the forest. The bullet left the casing housed in the chamber and raced forward through the barrel. It hit the open air; expanded as it crossed the short distance; slammed into, penetrated, tore out the opposite side of the boy's head. Brain matter spilled on to the forest floor.

For a brief second there was silence.

Utter, irrevocable, silence.

The leader snatched the gun from his hand, backed away and pointed it at Karl. 'Don't get any more ideas, brave man. You're done working for today.'

Several boys ran into the clearing to investigate the gunfire.

Karl was still staring at the boy.

'Did he shoot at you?' one asked.

Karl didn't move.

'Take him to the truck,' the leader ordered. 'And bring shovels back when you're done.'

A boy stepped forward and grabbed Karl's arm.

Hours later, huddled in the back of the truck, the boys

continued their journey. The driver slowed when they came upon a column of Jews being forced to march west, away from abandoned concentration camps further east that the Russians were closing in on. Karl stuck his head out of the window and looked at the line stretching to the horizon.

The boy had escaped from the column, Karl thought. He had reached the trees. He had made it to a grove. *He would have survived,* Karl muttered. *He would have survived.*

The truck jerked forward, knocking him to the floor. He felt ill. His stomach knotted. He lifted his head to stand up, then realised he was no longer in the truck, no longer surrounded by the boys, no longer near his leader. They were dead. Their truck was hit by a shell when they left him behind in Saxony. He was the only survivor. He fell down again and held his stomach. When he came to, he knew he had to pick himself up. His mother was waiting.

At a fork in the path, Karl shivered and glanced around the forest. He squeezed his eyes shut and asked God to prove He existed by placing him on the hill beside the church in Germau, so that when he opened his eyes he would see the village below as he remembered it – before it had descended into war. He promised God he would devote himself to Him for the rest of his life, if He fulfilled his prayer. He closed his eyes so tightly that he began to see colours and bursts of light. When he opened them, he was standing in the same place. He meditated on the boy he had murdered, shutting his eyes again to ask God to forgive him, before abandoning his prayer, no longer certain God existed.

He looked into the dark forest once again, then took the left fork in the path. He walked as fast as possible. He sensed something was watching him. He knew he could never be free. Even if he confessed to his mother, as she had pushed him to, how could he redeem himself for taking someone's life? Spirits glided through the trees around him. He promised himself that as soon as his mother was well enough he would tell her what he had done and ask her how he might atone for his crime.

Chapter 14

Instead of going to Partschefeld, he went straight to Jena and stopped at each health facility until he learned that his mother was being treated at the university hospital. When he arrived he was informed that Ida wasn't permitted visitors because of her deteriorating condition. Insisting he be allowed to see her, he was told that she was no longer conscious. When Karl asked what was wrong with her the nurse paused, then answered, 'Cancer. Women's cancer.' As Karl listened to her run through a litany of clinical explanations regarding his mother's condition, while thinking about what he had just confronted in the forest, the full realisation of his mother's fate fell upon him: she was dying.

After surviving the war, after surviving their separate journeys west, after surviving the surrender and escaping the widespread hunger that followed, after the reunion in the mountain village a short distance from Jena and making it through the events of the American withdrawal and the Russian takeover, after all the time that had passed when everything seemed to be moving forward, the very opposite had occurred. At first Karl refused to believe the nurse's prognosis. Even though she had avoided stating his mother's fate directly, the implication of her words was clear: Ida had little time left. It was unlikely that she would regain consciousness. Karl wondered if his mother's condition was God's punishment for him killing the boy.

The nurse told him that his aunt had gone back to Partschefeld that morning to retrieve Ida's papers, but that she planned to return the following day. After the nurse had prepared him, she agreed to take him upstairs to see his mother. They climbed a staircase at the rear of the hospital and walked quietly along a corridor where the handful of passing doctors and nurses avoided looking at Karl. He had never been in a hospital before. The ceilings seemed unusually high, the hall far too long. The echoing click, click, click of the nurse's heels on the tiled floor made Karl think of his grandfather walking along the cobbled road on his wooden leg, before the vibration of a stainless-steel cart being pushed down the hallway distracted him. He watched the cart pass, bloodied surgical tools poking out from under the edge of the white towel covering them. Karl felt his senses deteriorating the further they went along the hallway – a few steps back the hallway had felt narrow, confining despite its high ceiling, but now its width seemed too great, as though they were crossing an immense room, with doorways along the walls leading into different wards. He could hear people moaning, but their diminishing groans seemed less like calls for help than unintelligible final confessions.

Before they reached the room, the nurse paused and gave him time to regain his composure. Even though they stopped for only a few seconds, the break in their rhythm made Karl feel weak. The nurse asked if he was all right. Karl nodded and followed her to a bed in the far corner. The woman lying there hardly looked like his mother – she was frail, her cheeks hollow, her face that of a person who had abandoned herself to death. Even her hair looked different, wet with sweat, unkempt and combed hastily back over her head. But he knew it was his mother, if only by her gently pointed chin and the shape of her nose. He glanced at her body covered by a sheet. She had always been thin, but the sheet covering her seemed too close to the mattress. His eyes returned to her face. He knew she wouldn't be pleased with the way the staff had combed her hair, but he decided not to say anything to the nurse since he was sure Elsa would fix it when she came back.

Karl reached out and touched her face. Then, self-conscious, he pulled back his hand, before instinctively reaching out a second time for her arm lying on top of the sheet alongside her body. The nurse stood a few feet away without saying anything. He ran his hand down her forearm, stopped at her hand and turned it over, exposing her palm. He glanced at it, then slid his own palm across hers and gently interlocked his fingers.

When the nurse saw a tear sliding down Karl's cheek she became self-conscious herself and shifted on her feet, the sound of her heels distracting Karl. He glanced back. She nodded that she'd wait in the hallway. He listened to her footsteps crossing the room and fall silent. He looked at the door to make sure the nurse wasn't watching, then turned to his mother, bent down, kissed her on the cheek and whispered, 'Please forgive me.'

He straightened up so no one would catch him talking to her. As he did so he noticed the window for the first time since entering the room. An enormous linden tree stood in the court-yard, under whose limbs a doctor was flirting with two nurses. He lowered his head in prayer at the sight of the linden so close to his mother; he thought she had probably asked to be placed by a window that overlooked the tree. At the same moment he began to understand the song about Italy that she had made him memorise the last time he had seen her. He glanced a second time at the door to make sure the nurse wasn't there. Then, before going to join her in the hall, he bent down to his mother's ear, kissed its lobe and sang as softly as possible so that only his mother could hear:

> In Capri after the red sun sinks into the sea,
> And the pale crescent moon rises in the sky,
> The fishermen cast their nets off the bow.
> For only the stars can show the heavens,
> The path with pictures that every fisherman knows,
> As from boat to boat the old song rings out:
> Bella, bella Marie, remain faithful, bella, to me,
> I'll come back tomorrow morning early,
> If you promise never to forget me.

Chapter 15

When Elsa returned the next evening she found her nephew at the bedside, where the nurse had allowed him to pull up a chair. Both remained silent, but Karl could tell by his aunt's expression that she was relieved to find another family member at Ida's side. She came up behind him and rested her hand on his shoulder, then passed her fingers through his hair, and said, 'You're a good son.'

Karl stood up, offered the chair to her and went to find another. They sat beside each other in silence. They sometimes got up and went into the hall, ran errands for each other or found something to eat, but they rarely talked. Words had lost their weight, but they did glance at each other for support. It was only a matter of waiting.

Ida was no longer given medication, except for a small dose of morphine. 'To keep her comfortable,' the doctor said. She had stopped ingesting liquid two days earlier. The doctor said it would only be another day, two at most, before she came to rest. His choice of words struck Karl as odd, but at the same time he realised there was no proper way to speak of a person's death to the surviving family members – the event was too personal, too intimate to be fully comprehended by anyone except those who shared the dying person's memories.

When Ida's body started to shut down, Karl and Elsa rarely left the room. Her breathing became so faint that one of them occasionally stood up and leaned down, placing his or her ear close to her nose to listen for air seeping in and out. Sometimes they heard nothing at all, then unexpectedly she'd inhale. To prepare them, the doctor had told them what would happen when she died. The event, though, still embarrassed them. But the fact that Ida never went into convulsions, hardly shuddered at all, had made her end seem all the more anticlimactic and difficult to comprehend. Elsa wasn't sure what she had expected, but she had thought her sister's death would be more definitive than the room filling with an unpleasant odour as her bowels relaxed for the final time.

Chapter 16

After cleaning Ida up, the staff left her in the room with Karl and Elsa. They had to wait for the doctor, who was in surgery, to come and pronounce her dead before they could take her to the morgue. They took up their places at her bedside and let the fact that Ida was no longer alive sink in. Karl had an empty feeling, almost relief that he didn't have to watch his mother decline any more, but then felt bad for feeling relieved by her death. He felt even worse when he didn't cry. He was saddened, but in a remote way, as though someone else's mother had died. When the staff came to take her body, leaving Karl and Elsa standing alone beside the empty bed, Karl finally sensed the enormity of her loss.

They stood there, staring at the impression her body had left in the mattress. A breeze rustled through the leaves of the tree outside the window. Karl felt his aunt's hand on the small of his back and turned. She looked towards the door: it was time to leave.

That night, as he lay waiting for sleep to come, he realised that he'd never be able to talk to his mother about what he had done. As his eyes grew heavy, he wondered if he would ever tell anyone what had happened, now that she was dead. The loud report of the pistol whose trigger he had squeezed made him jerk from his half-conscious state and stare wide-eyed at the ceiling. Even if he had wanted to return to the place where he had murdered the boy to mark the grave and seek atonement for his crime, he knew it was impossible: he'd never find the place – he had no idea even where they had stopped that day.

What right did he have, he wondered, ever to return home to Samland or to preserve his culture when he had taken an active, personal role in destroying another? He stared at the ceiling, wondering what his future held, then thought again of the impression his mother's body had left in the mattress, wishing more now than ever that she were still here so that he could talk to her.

The day following Ida's death was so busy that there was little time to mourn. Without ever learning how the news had reached his father so fast, Karl answered the door that afternoon and saw him standing in the hallway. Paul marched around Jena acting like the boss, collecting the death certificate, thanking the doctor, paying for their meals and the room the three of them stayed in. While waiting out the week for the ashes, Elsa sent for the other children so the entire family could make the trip back to Partschefeld together. Paul's arrival was awkward, since Karl was the only one who had spent any time with him since the war. He was a complete stranger to Peter and Leyna. There was little family feeling or tenderness between them.

Paul busied himself balancing the books for his business whenever they had a break. He was uncomfortable adjusting to the fact that the children would soon be his responsibility. He did pick up Leyna sometimes and tell her how much she resembled her mother, but it was clear that he lacked the fathering skills Elsa assumed he once possessed. His presence made Elsa worry that her own husband's eventual return would be just as uncomfortable, but she reassured herself that her marriage shared few similarities with her sister's.

The following day the family walked to the coffin shop managed by an old man who also sold urns. The boys had asked if they could stay back at the room, but Elsa insisted they come to help pick it out. The coffin maker showed them one whose top was inlaid with amber. He knew the family was East Prussian by their accents and was aware that they might like amber. When he unexpectedly mentioned Palmnicken as the origin of the amber in the lid, Karl turned away and stared at the ground.

Without examining the urn further, Paul paid for it. As they waited for the man to finish wrapping it, Karl thought of Mr Wolff standing in front of his shop after the men had examined his identity card. He remembered the distant look in his eyes when he had glanced up and saw Karl staring at him through his bedroom window. Karl regretted not waving and wondered if he had missed an opportunity where he could have helped Mr Wolff. It occurred to him that if he had tried to help him in some way before it was too late, his own life might have taken a different path, instead of leading to the grove where he had shot the boy. But before he had a chance to consider the possibilities of missed opportunities further, Paul rushed the family out of the shop.

It was dusk by the time they left Jena. When the train dropped them off in Uhlstädt it was late at night – the sky black, except for a sliver of arched moonlight, whose tip dangled like a fish-hook in the sky. Instead of finding someone to carry them up the road to Partschefeld, Elsa suggested they walk the two kilometres.

The children glanced at the urn cradled in the crook of Paul's arm. Elsa led them into the forest along the narrow dirt road and up the slope, as the horses had their first time on the mountain. It was so dark that they bunched up as close together as possible. They had walked only a few hundred metres when Leyna began to cry. Elsa reached down, took hold of her hand and whispered, 'Be good for your mother.'

The air was crisp. Paul had on a long coat. The children wore scarves wrapped tightly round their necks. Every once in a while, Karl thought he heard something moving in the forest beside them. He didn't mention it but when he heard it again, he jumped and bumped into Peter. To keep from hearing more noises, Karl focused on their footsteps shuffling along the road. But even then he kept imagining an extra set walking beside them. He imagined his mother there with them, walking one last time through the forest with her family. He could see her smiling, the same delicate smile as on the afternoon he memorised the lyrics with her. He held the image in his mind to keep from becoming frightened as they climbed towards the village.

When they neared the edge of the forest and stopped to catch their breath, the dim outline of the chapel came into view. They paused a moment longer, then continued to the small cemetery. They went to the rear corner where Gerhard had dug a small hole. Paul set the urn on the ground. Each child knelt in turn, said a prayer and kissed the lid of the urn, followed by Elsa, who whispered a prayer and carefully placed it in the dark hole in the earth.

Karl wondered whether his mother was watching from above. He looked around as though hoping to catch a final glimpse of her, but saw only clouds blowing in from the Harz Mountains to the west. He wondered if she were encased in their mass, floating across the sky, free of the turmoil rooted to the ground below. He tried to imagine himself floating with her, reaching out to hold her hand as they drifted east. But each time he felt himself break free, his siblings' or aunt's crying distracted him. He looked at his aunt, covering her face with her hands. He moved towards her and nudged against her to comfort her, too inhibited to reach out. He glanced into the hole, imagining he had finally found the opening to the secret tunnel, as his father retrieved the shovel leaning against the fence. He knew he had to take something from that final meeting, something to claim, to hold as his own to ensure that his mother's last rites were preserved; it was her wish, he knew, that the family carry on, while remembering the journey that had brought them to her final resting place.

On the same afternoon that he had walked with her through the forest above the cemetery, listening to her singing about falling in love down in Italy, she had stopped near an opening in the forest. For a minute her face had become serious in a remote way he had never seen before. She had warned him not to fall into a lull, simply because they had survived their journey. 'Your journey's yet to begin,' she said. Then she had pointed at a distant ridge and told him to imagine a hundred more exactly like it behind the first. 'You can't see it,' she said. 'But you're going there.' She had paused, looked out at the ridge and continued, 'You can't go to a place and find happiness. That comes at the end, when you know you accomplished what you set out to do. You just have to go.' When he started to ask her a question, she had gently placed her fingertip on his lips, then leaned down, kissed him and started singing their song again.

Paul was now standing at Karl's side. Instead of filling the hole himself, while the family mourned, he held out the shovel to his son, waiting. Karl stood there for a time ignoring his father, aware that everyone else was ignoring him too. He looked up again at the clouds to see if they were still crossing the sky, but the only thing that drew his attention was his father's pointed stare. He reached out for the shovel, which Paul held on to, as if it were a game, before letting go. Karl fell backwards. He got up without looking at the sky or his father, plunged the shovel's blade into the soil piled beside the hole and began throwing dirt over the urn, gently enough to avoid breaking the ceramic but with sufficient force to keep himself from crying.

When he had finished filling the grave, he stepped back and looked up at the clouds again, which had now sealed the moon from view. For a brief second, between two merging clouds, he saw a stork with its wings outstretched, legs dangling behind. Peering into the darkening sky, he comprehended the full weight of his mother's advice: he could not simply remember parts of what had happened during the war, especially if one day he passed down the story of their journey west to his own children. He would have to tell them everything that had happened – everything, including what he had never been able to share with his own mother.

ACKNOWLEDGEMENTS

The Oscar Wilde Centre, Trinity College Dublin. Committee on Prizes, University of California Berkeley. Department of English, College of the Redwoods. In addition I owe a special debt of gratitude to the following:

My mother Jane Lavonne Keal, father Joachim Paul Malessa (1933-1998) and siblings, here and lost: Paul, Mark, Maria, Gretchen, Eddie, Brigitte and Peter. An especial thanks to my relatives Brigitte Maruna, Ulrich Malessa, Joachim Barlick and Siegfried Bayda.

The Susan Golomb Literary Agency (US), Abner Stein (UK). Interpreters Hans-Peter Schmidt-Treptow (Germany), Lidia Nebaba (Poland), Oleg Popov (Russia). Laura Tinari, Jeanne Akamine, Chris Hardwicke, Robert Brown & James Wiggins, Perry Kacprzak, Bill Salzmann, H.F. Christensen, The Sood family – Roopinder, Sandeep, Mona, et al., Bill Davenport, Mike Pucci, Jason Mitchell, James Peake, Elizabeth Phillips, Vernon Felton, Panagos Callas, Don Newroth, Ariane Simard, Catherine Heaney and Hyunh Thanh Ha.

ally, my editor Clare Reihill without whom this project would ssible.

Author's Note: The historical events on which this novel is based come from numerous sources – scholarly, archival, museums, interviews, personal histories, etc – as well as physical research at each location herein described. While the historian is not a novelist, neither is the novelist a historian. Sequence and locations are occasionally altered slightly to suit story.

ACKNOWLEDGEMENTS

The Oscar Wilde Centre, Trinity College Dublin. Committee on Prizes, University of California Berkeley. Department of English, College of the Redwoods. In addition I owe a special debt of gratitude to the following:

My mother Jane Lavonne Keal, father Joachim Paul Malessa (1933-1998) and siblings, here and lost: Paul, Mark, Maria, Gretchen, Eddie, Brigitte and Peter. An especial thanks to my relatives Brigitte Maruna, Ulrich Malessa, Joachim Barlick and Siegfried Bayda.

The Susan Golomb Literary Agency (US), Abner Stein (UK). Interpreters Hans-Peter Schmidt-Treptow (Germany), Lidia Nebaba (Poland), Oleg Popov (Russia). Laura Tinari, Jeanne Akamine, Chris Hardwicke, Robert Brown & James Wiggins, Perry Kacprzak, Bill Salzmann, H.F. Christensen, The Sood family – Roopinder, Sandeep, Mona, et al., Bill Davenport, Mike Pucci, Jason Mitchell, James Peake, Elizabeth Phillips, Vernon Felton, Panagos Callas, Don Newroth, Ariane Simard, Catherine Heaney and Hyunh Thanh Ha.

Finally, my editor Clare Reihill without whom this project would not be possible.

Author's Note: The historical events on which this novel is based come from numerous sources – scholarly, archival, museums, interviews, personal histories, etc – as well as physical research at each location herein described. While the historian is not a novelist, neither is the novelist a historian. Sequence and locations are occasionally altered slightly to suit story.